# Dafydd ap Gwilym

## Paraphrases and Palimpsests

Giles Watson

© 2014 Giles Watson. All rights reserved.
**ISBN** 978-1-291-86680-3

# Table of Contents

## Preface
## Love-bowers
*The Girl-Goldsmith* 12
*My Court of Broom* 13
*The Birchwood House* 16
*The Haycock* 17
*The Tree-Man* 18
*A Guildhall of Leaves* 20
*The Ruin* 22
*The Wounded Thorn*

## Love protested
*Faithfulness* 28
*Morfudd Like the Sun* 29
*Despondency* 31
*Loving a Nun* 32
*Dyddgu* 33
*Under the Eaves* 35
*Fighting for Morfudd* 37
*Love Pangs* 39
*The Melody* 41
*Her False Oath* 43
*That Near-Nun from Eithinfynydd* 44
*Nun-Baiting* 45
*The Greeting Unspoken* 47
*The Nocturnal Lovers Part at Dawn* 48

## Love messengers
*The Song Thrush* 52
*The Roebuck* 53
*The Seagull* 55
*The Greenwood Mass* 56
*The Titmouse* 58
*The Trout* 60
*A Dream from Annwn* 62
*The Salmon* 64
*The Swan* 67
*The Woodcock* 69
*The Blackbird* 71
*Beseeching St. Dwynwen* 73

*A Shriek of Blodeuwedd*    75
*The Crow*    77

## Love hindered

*The Owl*    80
*The Fox*    82
*The Frown*    84
*The Untameables*    85
*The Magpie's Counsel*    87
*The Clock*    89
*The Goose Shed*    91
*The Spear*    93
*The Window*    95
*The Peat-Pit*    97
*Love's Tilth*    99
*The Bramble*    101
*Trouble at a Tavern*    103
*The Enchantress*    105

## Love triumphant

*A French Kiss*    110
*Playing 'Nuts In My Hand'*    112
*Clandestine Love*    115
*Englynion on a Kiss*    116
*A Garland of Peacock Plumes*    117
*The Cuckold and the Cuckoo*    118
*Yesterday*    119

## Love fading

*The Poet Goes Floppy*    124
*Sore Trials of Love*    125
*Her Beauty Spoiled*    127
*The Cuckoo Pays a Debt*    127

## The elements

*The Enchanted Mist*    130
*The Star*    132
*The Wind*    134
*Cywydd for the Stars*    136
*The Ice*    139
*The Moon*    143
*Lost in the Mist*    144
*The Deluge*    146

## The seasons

*May and January* — 150
*The Leafy Bower* — 152
*May Month* — 153
*In Praise of Summer* — 155
*The Holly Grove* — 157
*Stealing Summer* — 159
*Winter-Courting* — 160
*Cywydd to the Snow* — 162
*Summer* — 164

## Self-evaluations

*The Heart* — 168
*The Mirror* — 170
*Englynion: Lament for Greying Hair* — 171
*Love Like a Fowler* — 172
*Needles in the Eye* — 174
*My Shadow* — 176
*A Dozen Reasons for Preferring a Poet to a Soldier* — 178
*Love's Journeyman* — 180
*The Funeral of the Poet, Killed Outright by Love* — 182
*Disputing with a Dominican* — 184
*The Sigh* — 186
*The Penis* — 187

## Satires

*Satire on Rhys Meigen* — 190

## Poems of Praise

*Thanks for the Gloves* — 194
*Basaleg* — 196
*Cywydd for Ifor Hael* — 198

## Elegies

*Elegy for Madog Benfras* — 202
*Elegy for Gruffudd ab Adda* — 204
*Rhydderch's Elegy* — 206
*Elegy for Dafydd ap Gwilym* by Iolo Goch — 208

## Epilogue

*Recanting* — 212

# *Preface*
## by Giles Watson

Dafydd ap Gwilym was an extraordinarily skilled poet, but he remains little known outside his native Wales. This is not because he wrote in the fourteenth century, for Chaucer was his contemporary. He is comparatively obscure because he wrote in Welsh, but it is also true that he achieved the greatest heights of artistry for the same reason. Whilst his poetry was not as ambitious in scope as Chaucer's, it presented a greater technical challenge. He most often wrote in *cywyddau*, couplets of seven syllables each, but the lines themselves were also given *cynghanedd* (harmony): complex sequences of alliterations, consonances, assonances and half-rhymes[1]. No living language is as perfect for such treatment as Welsh. The effect is mesmeric, frequently with the force of an incantation, and must have been more so with a harp accompaniment: an instrument with which Dafydd himself was proficient. It is also an effect which is virtually impossible to achieve in English translations – and indeed, most of Dafydd's translators have not attempted to do so.

The poems contained in this booklet are not translations. Readers will find excellent and exact prose renderings of Dafydd's best poems in Rachel Bromwich's scholarly and sensitive *Dafydd ap Gwilym: A Selection of Poems*, Helen Fulton's *Dafydd ap Gwilym: Apocrypha*, and in Kenneth Hurlstone Jackson's *Celtic Miscellany*, and some very effective verse renderings in Gwyn Thomas's *Dafydd ap Gwilym: His Poems*[2], although none of these attempt to reproduce Dafydd's metrics[3]. Indeed, I am not qualified to offer any sort of translation – merely homage to the poet in English, borne out of a lifelong obsession. Many, but not all of them retain his seven syllable lines[4], but I have found it necessary to resort to

---

[1] In a famous footnote, Robert Graves endeavoured to illustrate *cynghanedd* in English in *The White Goddess*: "Billet spied,/ Bolt sped./ Across field/ Crows fled,/ Aloft, wounded,/ Left one dead." He admitted, however, that the attempt was unsatisfactory.

[2] Rachel Bromwich, *Dafydd ap Gwilym: A Selection of Poems*, Gomer Press, Ceredigion, 1982; Helen Fulton, *Dafydd ap Gwilym: Apocrypha*, Gomer Press, Ceredigion, 1996; Kenneth Hurlstone Jackson, *A Celtic Miscellany: Translations from the Celtic Literature*, Penguin Books, Harmondsworth, 1971; Gwyn Thomas, *Dafydd ap Gwilym: His Poems*, Cardiff, 2004. Further literal translations of the poems may be found at www.dafyddapgwilym.net.

[3] The metre of eight of Dafydd's poems is elegantly preserved in translations by Anthony Conran (*The Penguin Book of Welsh Verse*, Penguin Books, Harmondsworth, 1967, pp. 137-150), but in terms of the shades of meaning offered by the originals, these are necessarily limited interpretations, though very perceptive and poetic ones.

[4] Those which do not are the poems which I paraphrased earliest. Whilst they do not preserve Dafydd's syllabics as effectively as my more recent paraphrases, I decided to retain them unedited in this edition, because for me, they have a sense of freshness of discovery which would be destroyed by re-working. These earlier attempts are: 'The Birchwood House', 'The Haycock', 'The Ruin', 'Morfudd Like the Sun', 'Despondency', 'Dyddgu', 'Her False Oath', 'The Song Thrush', 'The Roebuck', 'The Greenwood Mass', 'The Titmouse', 'A Shriek of Blodeuwedd', 'The Owl', 'The Magpie's Counsel', 'The Crow', 'The Clock', 'The Spear', 'The Enchanted Mist', 'May and January', 'The Leafy Bower', 'May Month', 'In Praise of Summer', 'The Holly Grove' and 'The Mirror'.

simple rhyming couplets rather than Dafydd's more complex, unrhythmical rhyming system, in which an accented final syllable rhymes with an accented one. The strict consonantal echoes of Welsh *cynghanedd* are replaced by much looser patterns of assonance, consonance and alliteration. Dafydd's characteristic habit of interjecting descriptions, images or exclamations in parenthetic phrases, known as *sangiadau*, also presents particular problems for the translator, and I have retained these at my own discretion. Mediaeval Welsh poetry also commonly draws on strings of metaphorical comparisons, or *dyfalu*. Sometimes these comparisons are unfavourable, and the poem takes the form of a satire or a curse. On other occasions, they are the means by which the poet pours his praises on an admired person or object. Because these sections are often the most energetic and humorous, it has often been necessary to seek alternative metaphors which "work" in English, although I hope that in doing so, I have remained true to the spirit, if not the literal meaning, of the originals.

The enduring appeal of Dafydd's poems is partly attributable to the universality of his themes, but it is his distinctively Welsh voice and his remarkable powers of observation which make him utterly compelling. Brought up in the thoroughly Christianised culture of mediaeval Wales, Dafydd was quite as capable as his English contemporaries when it came to writing poems of penitence, or *englynion* rehearsing Christian doctrine - yet he did not forget his country's pagan roots, and referred to the heroes and cosmology of the *Mabinogion* and the *Trioedd Ynys Prydain* with the same reverence he demonstrated for God, Mary (transliterated in my paraphrases as Mair) and the saints. He was also emotionally honest to the point of blasphemy: invoking saints for assistance in illicit love affairs, venting his frustration at his rejection in love by announcing his intention to seduce the local abbess, and populating his woodlands with birds wearing vestments of feathers, serving at a Mass in which the consecrated wafer was a fallen leaf.

Dafydd invented, followed, and flouted a range of conventions. First, there are the poems in which the speaker claims to have constructed an abode in the greenwood, suitable for clandestine trysting with his beloved. The covert nature of the assignation is nearly always necessitated by the fact that the beloved is married to someone else – a cuckold who is commonly named *Eiddig* – or because the speaker has not met the approval of the girl's father. Often, it seems, this background is mere scaffolding on which to hang a poem in praise of nature, and in one case, ('The Wounded Thorn'), *Eiddig* plays an active part in destroying the greenwood trysting-tree. It seems very likely, however, that Dafydd was also writing from personal experience, and it is easy to believe that the two named lovers in his poems – the dark-haired Dyddgu and the blonde-haired Morfudd – really existed. We have it on Dafydd's authority that he first met Morfudd at a mystery play in Bangor Cathedral, but despite his ceaseless protestations of love, it seems that she married another, and that her husband was violent towards her. Dafydd made verse appeals for the approval of Dyddgu's father, but does not appear to have received it. Other lovers go unnamed, or are compared with the radiant beauties of Welsh mythology, such as Enid, Luned and Gwinevere.

The *llatai* convention appears to have been Dafydd's own invention, and is the main subject of a number of his poems, some of which testify to his skills as an observer of nature. These involve the poet addressing an animal, or even an elemental force such as the wind, with a request to carry a message to his beloved. One at least one occasion, Dafydd receives a *llatai* from his lover – as opposed to sending one out himself – and in one case, the *llatai* is revealed in a dream. These poems have their own peculiar magic, and are undoubtedly rooted in the shape-shiftings of Welsh mythology. For this reason, I have included Dafydd's poem about that archetypal shape-shifter, Blodeuwedd, in the section on love-messengers. The sympathetic tone of this poem is in marked contrast with another poem on 'The Owl', which introduces some of the love messengers who are cursed by Dafydd for bringing bad news. Not only mammals and birds serve as love-messengers; the elements and heavenly bodies do so too, and again, sometimes they are blessed, and sometimes cursed, by Dafydd.

Perhaps it is not surprising - given that the illicit nature of Dafydd's love affairs required him to hold his trysts in the cover of the greenwood - that Dafydd wrote a number of poems in which he extolled the virtues of the summer months, and scorned the winter. Some of these poems extol a natural spirituality which is refreshing in its simplicity. These are balanced by more introspective poems in which Dafydd either argues with himself, his shadow (or, in one notorious case, a part of his anatomy), or becomes embroiled in a disputation with a friar. Here, honesty is combined with a humorous self-irony which modern readers ought to find endearing. Dafydd was also an inimitable satirist, and there is even a tradition which asserts that Rhys Meigen dropped dead on the spot when the poem which lampoons him was recited. Finally, there are the poems in which Dafydd extols the virtues of powerful men; sometimes in the form of praise poems, and just as often in the form of elegies, many of which were written long before the subject died. It seemed fitting to round off the collection with my own deliberately loose paraphrase of Iolo Goch's elegy to Dafydd himself.

Much paper has been wasted – and much academic energy fruitlessly expended – in debating which poems attributed to Dafydd ap Gwilym by the manuscripts ought actually to belong to the 'canon', ever since Thomas Parry first suggested one in his *Gwaith Dafydd ap Gwilym* (1952). Although I have mentioned some of these controversies in my notes at the end of each poem, my opinions are based on instinct alone. Some poems which are quite obviously Dafydd's work, such as 'The Penis', were excluded by Parry for moralistic reasons. Others were excluded because he regarded their metrical structures as not being strict enough: a dubious criterion, in my opinion, given Dafydd's penchant for defying conventions, even when he had invented them. The existence of two poems on an identical theme (such as those describing a would-be lover lost in the mist) complicates matters still more. It is certainly true that other poets passed their work off as Dafydd's own, but the mediaeval notion of authorship was not as fixed as ours, and the criteria by which I have made my selection are not scientific. On one occasion ('The Blackbird'), I have included a poem which I am convinced is the work of a later author, simply because it is so clearly influenced by Dafydd, and because it contains some interesting features which resonate with the poems I have gathered around it.

There are, however, certain features which – whilst they cannot be said to constitute litmus tests for Dafydd's authorship – would certainly help to earn Dafydd's own stamp of approval. They are: a refusal to allow the strictures of any moral or religious code to impede poetic sympathy for a person who is in love (a tendency which Dafydd inherits from the troubadours and perhaps Marie de France), a selfless and unswerving devotion to beauty, a preference for the natural over the artificial, an acute capacity for the close observation of nature, and most importantly, a generous helping of self-irony. There is nothing surprising or unique in this. These are, in fact, the most fundamental characteristics of any poet who deserves the name. What is unique is Dafydd's distinctive voice. I cannot begin to explain how it sounds, but I know it when I hear it, and if these paraphrases can catch even an echo of it, I am well pleased.

# Love-bowers

## *The Girl-Goldsmith*
Yr Euryches

Girl-goldsmith of the garland-
Circlet of birch leaves, her gold
Gleaned from twigs – a woodland gift,
Gain of patience, goodly graft,
Gilt through craft of growth and love
In her smithy of glittering leaves –
Garners praise: molten silver.
Love's ardour is her solder.
Her beauty is the treasure
Where dew drips like a tear,
A gem distilled, fed by roots,
Garland twisted from the shoots
Growing in the hilltop grove.
She twists, winds. Her hand engraves
Bright sigils to bind my heart,
Thumb and finger keeping hold
Of each wire. Fire of amber
Glows like a dying ember
In a torc or tarnished brooch.
More beautiful by far: birch
Woven like wicker. True worth
Is her troth, knit in a wreath.

I treasure my birch garland –
Tortured by such hard longing –
Hold it to my heart. It hurts
To clutch it through summer's heat,
But I am bound by it. Cool
Autumn refines it. How cruel,
Her art! More fool me - trusting
To twigs of Morfudd's twisting,
My breast riven by desire,
Smelted with her summer-fire.
Skilful witching! By my word,
She works jewels out of wood,
To shame Siannyn! My praise
And slavery is the price.
Lucky is the man who finds
Himself in the woods, entwined
Between her enamel legs,
Enmeshed in her twist of twigs.

## *My Court of Broom*
Llys y Banhadlwyn

Royalty of hue and form
She has – maid of regal fame –
Woe to him who cannot taste
Her lips, or arrange a tryst
With her, by day forbidden
To approach my Moon Maiden.
God condemns these trysts by night
Behind some wall, evading sight!

A green court for embraces:
Tangled basket of branches:
Too long to wait for summer's grace
To make green our trysting place,
So God gave me, in the cold,
Royal trees in robes of gold,
Winter twigs as hale and green
As verdure in summer's sheen.
There, of broom I make a bower
Enchanting as a wizard's tower,
A hall such as Merlin made
Of glass in a crystal glade
For Vivien. Like the veil
That hung on Dyfed, fey, pale,
Is the roof my ardour weaves
Of golden flowers and growing leaves.
And should she come, my countess
To my gilt-strewn thatch, I'll bless
Her gleaming hair, and thrice
Kiss her in our Paradise
Of woven twigs, and leaves fresh
As sweet lovers' nubile flesh.

Lincoln green, the leaves of May
Bring dignity to each spray;
Flowers of gold on silken threads
Hang where lissom footfall treads.
Luxuriant, spreading tree,
Tipped with gold, as fair as she
Who comes: each branch a bright rod,
A sceptre in the hand of God!
May she thrill in sylvan heaven
As Eve in a poet's Eden.
Praise and poesy bright have spun
Yellow frost distilled from sun.

My maiden's mane will toss there
Like horses at a saffron fair,
A house of leaf in summer's sight
Suffused with Arabian light,
Tabernacle of the Lord,
Jewelled like the roof that soared
Above the angels in flight,
Embroidered all with May's delight.
Gossamer of gold, and bees,
Bright butterflies, sunshine's beads.
I am a mage with golden touch;
I make each branch glow: a torch,
A chapel which the wind tosses,
Studded all with stellar bosses.
Like tiny birds of May, they perch
About the rafters of my church,
Mair's candles all alight,
Marigolds that dazzle sight.
Behold my grove: dome of pleasure
Crammed full with angels' treasure
Enough to charm a Cheapside shop:
Trinkets grown of Sunday's crop.

Sitting in my grove I wait:
She is fashionably late.
I'm committed; I'll not blench,
But canopied, await the wench,
For I can bear with winter's mist
If summer gives me but one tryst!
Come, my slim girl! There's room
For coupling in my Court of Broom.

**Notes:** In the mediaeval period, this was sometimes attributed to Robin Ddu (fl. 1450), and more often to Dafydd ap Gwilym, but modern scholars have suggested that it is a fifteenth century imitation. Broom branches are green all the year round, and the plants may be found in flower much earlier than most others. The royal dynasty of the Plantagenets take their name from the broom, long known in Latin as the *Planta genista*. Henry II wore a spray of broom in pod as a badge, and almost certainly, the Plantagenets acquired the name when it was first applied to Henry's father, Geoffrey, Count of Anjou: a fitting title, because Anjou and neighbouring Brittany are covered with broom bushes. Broom has long had a reputation as a magical plant, partly because of its beauty, but also because of the intoxicating and mildly hallucinogenic properties of its flowers, which were added to beer to give it an extra kick, and used in the spell which made Blodeuedd in the *Mabinogion*. Witches and fairy queens have long been associated with broom, as they are in the ballads 'Broomfield Hill' and 'Tam Lin'. (For further details, see Geoffrey Grigson, *The Englishman's Flora*, St. Alban's, 1975, pp. 138-140.) 'Dafydd' makes his broom grove into a scene of enchantment by comparing it with the glass castle in which Merlin courted Vivien (or, more commonly, was imprisoned by her), and by his reference to the enchantment of Dyfed in the days of Pryderi and Manawydan in the Third Branch of the *Mabinogion*. Such a comparison is appropriate, because the enchantment of Dyfed caused all other human beings to unaccountably disappear: perfect conditions, surely, for a lovers' tryst. These metaphors stand in self-ironic contrast to some of the more worldly comparisons, such as the

Cheapside shop and the fairground. I have extended this hint of self-irony – so typical of Dafydd's amorous verse – by means of a sudden lapse into coarseness in the final section of the poem.

# *The Birchwood House*
Y Ty Bedwen

I love a long, lithe blonde
Whose will I cannot bend –
Frustrated at every meeting,
Led on by her sweet mocking –
A devious, murmuring girl
Diverting me from my goal:
"I love not your impropriety.
You knave! You own no property!"

By her curt words spurned
I thought I understood:
I built, in a grove of birch,
A house beneath a branch,
Finely plaited with praise,
A structure of grace and poise
Roofed with sticks and twigs
With layered leaves for tiles –
A house meet for lovers
With two faithful lodgers:
Cock thrushes, dapple-breasted.
With sparkling songs, they boasted
Loud as Eden's birds,
Two garrulous, gifted bards,
Who each day, from the house
Seven songs rehearsed
To woo the maiden's ear.
I listened. Was she near?

She came not, though I willed it.
She knows not I have built it.

Unless some maid shall wend
Her way into my wood
I'll build no birchwood gable
Again for any girl.

**Notes:** All sixteen manuscripts of this poem attribute it to Dafydd ap Gwilym.

# *The Haycock*
Y Mwdwl Gwair

Loitering by my lover's lair
Lying sleepless in her allure;
It's hard to balance loss and gain
Lovelorn and sluiced with rain.
Had she left an open door
For me, alas I would not dare
To enter, fearing her reproof –
Haycock, be my walls and roof.

Haven haycock, tousled stack,
Green of head, pale and stark:
Praise the rake that worked to gather
Every severed stalk together.
I am a bard in green raiment
Wearing hay: a graceful garment.
I dug a hole here. Like dove
In columbarium, sick with love.
Meadow grass cut limp and long
Here I languish, lost in song.

Like a barrow you were built
And each skein of grass was bent
As if to chamber some great lord,
And like a lord you suffer. Sword-
Sharp iron left you slain
But you bleed without a stain.
Tomorrow, ere the light has failed
They'll have dragged you from the field.
Mair have mercy! They'll hang you high
Above dry stubble, there to die.

I pray you find your rest, and lie
In the hayloft. Watch me fly
An angel over close-mown land
When the Judgement is at hand:
"Haycock, now the time is right
For stalk and soul to reunite."

**Notes:** One of Dafydd's strangest poems, this appeals to the animist in me. It bears comparison with 'The Ruin' since both the haycock and the ruin are structures whose transience is lamented by the poet, and both of them are seen to have personalities of their own. Modern folkies may notice affinities with 'John Barleycorn'.

## *The Tree-Man*
Y Gwialwr

I made a tryst, by my troth
With she who never tells truth,
In sylvan house, strewn with vines,
I await her there in vain.

A house I built, for my witch,
Of leaves, then set fruitless watch,
Overgrown my oak-tree grove,
Lapped by lakes, a living grave.
In summertime, I like to trust
Her wilful ways to keep the tryst:
Upon each branch, buds will break,
Midsummer on the brink
Of dawning. I am blessed:
Twenty summers I can boast
Without once, as I live,
Having lied regarding love:
How? I'm silent. But how sharp
Her lies – alas, she won't shut up!
I spoke, yet she paid no heed,
Acting like she had not heard.

I first made tryst with Madam
When the dust was made Adam;
I have waited five long lives,
Face wrapped with the hedgerow leaves,
Parched by sun, drenched by rain,
No man living knows such pain:
There are trees, great-girthed, that grow
Perforce above me. Frost, snow
Have barked my skin, rough and raw
As rind of lowland's withered haw –
'A tree-man', so they say, 'No jest,
Or some poor saint put to test.
Gwernabwy's eagle; stone clutcher,
Is not so old; no creature
Waits as long. No Stag giving counsel
Nor Cilgwri's ancient Ousel.
Llyn Llyw's Salmon was small fry;
Cwm Cawlwyd's owl too young to fly.'

Know, girl, love grows from my girth
Like Aaron's rod thrust in the earth,
And when I lie down, I shall root
In my own grave. A quickened shoot

Cannot be buried in the mould,
Though I'm gnarled and grim and old.
Whet a knife and cut them stark:
Her initials in my bark.
Engrave her picture where I lie,
Since I love, and cannot die.

**Notes:** Dafydd's authorship has been questioned, but the rich allusiveness of this poem certainly bears his trademarks: especially the manner in which references to the Old Testament are blended with folkloric motifs of more obviously pagan origin. The references to the creation of Adam and to Aaron's rod (Numbers 17), are balanced by a string of comparative hyperboles emphasising the length of the poet's waiting for his love. In Culhwch and Olwen, a tale from the Mabinogion, King Arthur's knights seek the whereabouts of Mabon son of Modron. Gwrhyr, the Interpreter of Tongues, speaks in turn to each of the Oldest Animals, enquiring as to Mabon's whereabouts. The Ousel of Cilgwri tells him that once there was a smith's anvil in the field, and the Ousel has been smashing snails and whetting his bill on it ever since, so that it is now worn to the size of a nut, but he has never heard of Mabon. The Stag of Redynvre says that an oak sapling has grown old, died, and worn into a stump in his lifetime, but he has never heard of Mabon. The Owl of Cwm Cawlwyd says that he has lived to see three forests grow on the glen that is his home, and has seen all three uprooted, but he has never heard of Mabon. The Eagle of Gwern Abwy once perched on a rock which his talons have now worn to a pebble, but he has never heard of Mabon. Finally, the Eagle leads Gwrhyr to the Salmon of Llyn Llyw, apparently the oldest creature on earth, and only he knows where Mabon is imprisoned. I have attempted to iron out an apparent inconsistency: early on, the poet claims to have lived only for twenty summers, but he later implies that his tryst with his beloved took place in antiquity. No doubt the latter is a deliberate exaggeration, but I have chosen to suggest instead that the poet (long since transformed into a tree) has been silent for twenty years because his trunk has fallen and is now growing recumbent. I have never seen any analysis of this poem in discussions of the "Green Man", but whilst the poet's tone is clearly tongue-in-cheek, it is difficult to dismiss the idea that foliate carvings or illuminations may have played a part in his inspiration.

## *A Guildhall of Leaves*
Saernïaeth Dail

Golden girl, whose gentleness gleams
With her name, Gwen, upon leaves:
Come, behold the bard who loves
You endlessly under leaves!
I thatched a house: here she lives
Roofed and raftered all with leaves.
My shining one glints and glows
Tabernacled under leaves.
But like all men with tidy lives,
Eiddig comes, strips off the leaves,
Leaves us naked: Gwen grieves
Her dark husband tearing leaves.

The best building man contrives
Is a Guildhall built of leaves
Crowned with twigs and harvest sheaves,
Or better: green springtide leaves.
The nightingale sings and slaves,
Our servant nightly under leaves;
The blackbird, winged in dark sleeves
Sings of woodcraft through the leaves;
The thrush, with words learnt of trees
Is enchantress of the leaves;
The cuckoo with bowed head grieves,
Grey-clad sexton of the leaves;
The yaffle green: she receives
Her consecration in the leaves.
The populace of leaves streams
With sunlight: I'll not leave the leaves.

A herd of deer and oxen teems
Through the greenwood choir of leaves:
Each creature, wild, tame, receives
Sustenance by eating leaves.
Cloaked, or wearing shepherd's weeds,
Girls hesitate to wait while leaves
Enclose them. A girl conceives
Man's woe, not lingering in leaves.

I am outlawed, on my knees
Because Eiddig tore my leaves,
The nameless one no one sees,
A Jack-of-Kent protecting leaves.
I'll ask nothing, when she leaves,

Except for sun, and life, and leaves.

**Notes:** All but one of the manuscripts of this poem attribute it to Dafydd ap Gwilym, but it has been argued that it may be a fifteenth century imitation. The original presents a more or less insoluble problem for the translator: all of its lines end in words with the suffix "-ail", and most with the word "dail", or "leaves". It has therefore been necessary to blend rhymes and pararhymes in order to convey in English something of the tone of the original. The name "Gwen", meaning 'fair', is a conventional poet's name for the beloved, but Dafydd himself usually uses Morfudd, Dyddgu, or the Arthurian Eigr: a possible argument against his authorship. Eiddig is, however, Dafydd's usual name for his love rival – specifically the husband of the beloved. There are other arguments for Dafydd's authorship, such as the characteristically acute observation in the original that the nightingale sojourns in Wales "a hundred nights" each year. The cuckoo is described as a sexton because one of the duties of the mediaeval grave-digger was also to ring the church bell: a comparison between bird-life and sacred duty which resonates with another poem firmly within the Dafydd ap Gwilym canon: 'The Greenwood Mass'. The connection between a life in the greenwood and outlawry or exile is of course a common mediaeval theme, and one shared by others of Dafydd's poems. Jack-of-Kent is, amongst other things, a common folkloric name for an outlaw – a Welsh equivalent of Robin Hood – and readers wishing to explore this further are directed to Alex Gibbon's lively and readable treatment of the subject in *The Mystery of Jack of Kent and the Fate of Owain Glyndwr*, Stroud, 2004.

# The Ruin
Yr Adfail

*Dafydd:*
"Ruined shack with shattered gable
By the hills where lambs gambol:
Ramshackle wreck, source of shame
To those long gone who called you home.
Once hospitable, listless shambles,
Broken lintels, cascading shingles
Are grim rebukes to those who played
Within these walls. I stand appalled
By your plight, unsightly hovel –
I, who one sweet night-time's revel
Within that nook once held a girl,
And she so loving, lacking guile,
And shapely. Her voice intoned
Sweet love, limbs intertwined
With mine. Our arms seemed knit,
Like fate, within a seamless knot.
She slaked my lust like melting snow,
And I, her bard, bade nations know
Her beauty. By sleight of hand
I made her goddess as I held
Her, safe within your wooden walls –
Wide open now to frosts and squalls."

*The Ruin:*
"Mine is the grief; I bear the wound
Dealt by a dauntless, wild wind.
Out of the east, with a mournful wail,
A wind demolished the drystone wall;
Out of the south a wrathful ghoul
Ripped my roof off with a gale."

*Dafydd:*
"Only the wind? Can emptiness wreak
Destruction on your roof, and wreck
Each strut and spar? Then wind
Makes mockery of the world.
Why, in that corner stood my bed,
Where that black sow tends her brood!
Yesterday, we were alive
And you were shelter for our love.
Today your door hangs, hinges broken
And rafters lie amid the bracken.
Delusions all, those dreams of loving,

And Death makes dupes of all the living."

*The Ruin:*
"Though you're a ghost and I'm a wreck
You lived and loved. I've done my work."


**Notes:** The original only implies that the voice of Dafydd is that of a ghost; I have made this more explicit. Laments for ruined buildings formed an entire sub-genre of mediaeval Welsh poetry, but this is perhaps the most accomplished. Dafydd's authorship is undisputed.

# *The Wounded Thorn*
Y Draenllwyn

Hawthorn tree, lush and stately,
Gentle *llatai*, lorn, laudatory,
Wrapped in bark and greenly clad,
Armed with spears, my Covert Lad,
Ever-changing in your guise,
Loved of God, of manly size!
In May, a fleeting wonder grows:
Wearing precious summer snows,
Your branches bow, each serried
With an army thorned, then berried.

From your foe a warlike blow
Has wedged deep: a cleft of woe:
Not half of you – not a third –
Remains to shelter beast or bird.
Star-Cherry, my living charm,
He cleaved your legs, meaning harm
To heartwood, bole, branch and leaf.
Say, Foam-Flower, who brought you grief?

"I am weak. I creak and sigh.
He came to me – I don't know why –
A wretched churl, axe-wielding fool,
Just yesterday. The blade cruel:
An axe with shaft of apple-wood.
He came to wound me where I stood
And spill my gems, shake my top,
In hopes my very crown to drop."

Such coral beads I have seen:
Jewels to crown an English queen!
Stand still, Soldier. By my verse
I'll win justice. Mortal curse:
The churl shall hang, a grave his bed;
By this song he'll swing, dog-dead.

**Notes:** Whilst it has been acknowledged that the poem is in a fourteenth century style, modern critics have suggested that it is not skilful enough to retain a definite place in the Dafydd ap Gwilym canon. The theme of the churlish love-rival (usually named Eiddig) who is also an over-enthusiastic hedge-cutter is, however, a favourite of Dafydd's, and is further evidence of the eternal relevance of his concerns. The choice of a tree as a *llatai* is also intriguing, since for obvious reasons, most of Dafydd's love messengers are highly mobile. Perhaps the tree was an appointed place for leaving hidden letters. A particularly charming feature of the poem is the gradual accumulation of the poet's affectionate nicknames for the tree, emphasising the fact that he knew it as an individual. The Hawthorn tree has snow-white blossoms in May, which are succeeded in the autumn by coral-coloured berries. In the right light, these are indeed jewel-like in appearance, and Dafydd's original makes an ironic comparison between the beauty of the berries and the jewels available – to those who could afford them – in an Englishman's shop. There is a bitterness to this line which is lost on modern audiences (Dafydd is thinking of the fact that after the Edwardian settlement of 1284, English settlers had the monopoly on urban trade), so I have replaced it with the more obvious, and equally ironic reference to "an English queen". Poets were more highly respected in mediaeval Celtic cultures than they are in our own, and it was believed that a poet's satires literally had the power to kill. As a result, the final lines of the poem can be seen as rather more than a mere expression of impotent rage. By coincidence, on the day I paraphrased this poem, I walked to a favourite patch of woodland, thick with gigantic ash trees and poplars, only to discover that every tree had been chain-sawed to the ground. My own rage may indeed be impotent, but I must confess that I shared Dafydd's feelings exactly.

# Love protested

## *Faithfulness*
Ffyddlondeb

I'll never let splendid Morfudd alone – sweet bird –
Although the Roman Pope groans
Over my sin. Her sunlit face atones
'Til honey oozes out of stones.

# *Morfudd Like the Sun*
Morfudd fel yr Haul

Girl! Soft-spoken, golden
Gleaming snow-strewn garden,
Gods know she is glowing,
Good as sea-foam gliding,
Girt by salt-strand glistening,
Gracious sunshine glancing,
Gleaning lovelorn garlands,
Gaining sun-strewn glories.
Goddess, sable-girdled,
Gilded husband-goader.
Great Morfudd, poet's grief,
Guide to my gaping grave,
Gilt hair of gossamer.
Girls turn men to ghosts.

Miraculous her deceptions,
Measureless mirth. My dear's
So fickle: now in church,
Now in court. I'll catch
Her on the battlements. Alas,
She disappears. Her loss
A sinking, like the sun
Depriving all of song:
Springtime's brightness,
May-day's brilliance.
Splendid gaudy Morfudd,
Bright sun of glistering Mair.

To the earth's wide brim
She descends. Her beam
Is dauntless day,
Shepherdess of sky.
Clouds come, waging war,
Across her face a shawl
Of stifling black, and soon
We pine for dazzling sun.
But darkness interposes:
At night-time she escapes,
Black smoke pollutes
The firmament of blue.
God's orb has gone,
And will she come again?
No hand can touch her;
No man can teach her
To stay. Tomorrow

She burns away sorrow.

Morfudd too has set
On me, as if to test
The troth that I have sworn
While she lights Annwn.
My sun is down once more
Behind her husband's door.

In Penrhyn's gleaming glade
I sought her, bright as gold:
Daily there she shines
And every night absconds.
Nor can I waylay
Her in the hall by day,
Or grab her by the shin
(Far easier grasp the sun)
But she outshines its form
With her flickering flame.
No wonder all men stare
For she outshines the stars.

Were she to come my way
By night, and make display,
The lesser sun could stay
To illuminate the day.
Throughout the world, the night
Would banished be from sight,
And darkness should take flight,
Ere she lives, from light.

**Notes:** It is quite impossible to do justice in English to this masterpiece of mediaeval verse. I have stuck to trimeter, although the original is more complex. In order to give some notion of the rich texture of this poem, I have preserved the heavy alliteration of the opening stanza, but not the *cynghanedd*, since this is seemingly impossible in English. The decision to revert to rhymes rather than pararhymes for the final stanza is my own and not the poet's, but it does reflect an intensification of sound patterns at the end of the original poem. Along with 'Love's Husbandry', this poem attests to Dafydd's ability to sustain a conceit with an effortlessness which would be the envy of any metaphysical poet, although one might expect a Donne or Crashaw to be rather scandalised by the suggestion that Morfudd's beauty rivalled that of the Virgin Mary ('Mair' in the original, and in all my paraphrases). The specific reference to Annwn (the Celtic underworld), whilst it does appear in other poems by Dafydd, is absent from this one, which speaks of the sun lighting the other side of the world. The rationale behind my using it here is based on a reading of Robert Graves's *The White Goddess* and the first branch of the *Mabinogion*. Morfudd returns to her husband by night, so by reading this as a descent to Annwn, I am suggesting that Morfudd's husband is the poet's weird or double, just as Arawn is Pwyll's weird in the *Mabinogion*.

# *Despondency*
Cystudd y Bardd

Careless Morfudd cast her spell
In mild May, my hopes to spoil.
I have no pride: I prate and plead
And waken in the night appalled.
She sowed her seed inside my breast;
It germinated. I was burst
Asunder, ripe for harvest.
She shone like sun. That was hardest:
Knowing she was witch and goddess
Beguiling me, and yet regardless,
Any libel she'd believe:
I'll gain no boon whilst I live.

This morning she was full of praise
And vaunted me above my peers;
Tonight I'm outlawed without trial,
Banished, cast upon the trail,
But when she reached within my heart
She planted tares too: longing, hurt.

As long as tides shall lap the shore
This outlaw hopes to have his share
Of Morfudd. Bound and fettered,
Sorrow-shackled, I have found
No peace with her, my golden girl,
But groan and grimace like a ghoul.
And now grown ill through cruel love
I doubt that I have long to live.

Ynyr's daughter is my dearth.
She has reaped me, sure as Death.

**Notes:** The poet's self-identification as an outlaw is significant, and is almost certainly also implied in those poems in which Dafydd constructs a greenwood retreat for his beloved.

## *Loving a Nun*
Caru Lleian

I'm off my food, lean for love:
A dark-eyed girl blights my life.
I must be mad: love behoves
Me, on Another One's behalf!
Long is my love, sore my hurt,
Biting like the fang of hate:
Woe to me Mair, should I lose
My girl, and deride my loss.

Can it be true? Would you spurn
My budding birches, and return
To sit inside that dour house
Telling beads, and then rehearse
Those psalms? Are you nun, or saint?
Choir's beloved, without taint,
Abjure bread and water. Christ
Commands: strive to give up cress.
Be done with beads, for Mair's sake,
And with carousing monks who seek
Your bounty. Do not be chaste
In springtime: get it off your chest!
I bet you blush beneath your veil,
Yet ring and mantle you revile.

Come within the birch tree court,
Join instead the cuckoo's cult!
High time it is that we strove
To reach for heaven in the grove.
Among the vines, atop the hill,
I shall atone, cheating hell.
God and the saints, as I'm alive,
Are sure (I hope) to pardon love.

**Notes:** All of the extant manuscripts name Dafydd as the author, or leave the author unnamed. An entire sub-genre was devoted to poems about wooing nuns, although few are quite as blatant as this one in its exhortation to leave the convent for the greenwood. The reference to "cress" is a taunt about the penitential monastic diet. Helen Fulton, *Dafydd ap Gwilym: Apocrypha* suggests that the line "Os myfi a'th gâr I arall" ought to be interpreted as "I love you just so someone else my win you". I have capitalised the reference to this personage, on the grounds that the poet appears to me to be jealous of the fact that the nun has taken vows as a "bride of Christ".

## *Dyddgu*
**(an appeal to her father)**
Dyddgu
(merch Ieuan ap Gruffud ap Llywelyn)

Ieuan with the spear of flame,
Gruffudd's son, of martial fame,
Fine your fortress, filled with wine,
Warlike chieftain! Zeal was mine:
Ebullient mood, bold delight,
At your house the other night.
Since that time the hours creep;
I pine away, deprived of sleep.
I indulged in all your wealth,
In sprightly wine drank your health.
Poured for poets: meady broth
Brimming with a head of froth!

Your daughter won't woo at all
Embattled in your solid hall.
I lose my words, I swoon, I leap,
Nor can I get a grip on sleep.
I can't escape, by prayer or art,
And nothing blooms within my heart
But love for her: a fond thought
Stifling other schemes to nought.
I age, I waste, uninvited:
All my love is unrequited.

My lithe darling would have daunted
Roman Magi, wise and vaunted:
Springtide snow; darkling fair,
White of brow with raven hair!
Bereft for love I am: the waste!
For the darkling girl is chaste –
Hair as black as ouzel's wing,
As polished jet, clasp or ring
About her white, unsullied throat –
Enough to make the angels gloat.

I, her poet, proclaim her prim,
Perfect form, by God's pure whim,
Is pert and plump enough to spur
The penchant of a Peredur:
Son of Efrog, fabled knight,
Dazzled by the burning light
Of sun on snow, eagle eyed,

Close by Esyllt's grove, espied
Upon a drift the flurried track
Of plunging hawk: smudge of black
Where the ouzel met its death,
Prone where talons stanched its breath –
Work of wrong – and yet by stealth
God has painted all the wealth
Of womanhood upon the snow:
The ouzel, black as any crow,
Flaps her eyelash in its throes,
The snow her brow. Thickly flows
The red blood, which spreads, seeps:
The setting sunlight of her cheeks.

Such is Dyddgu, crowned in gold,
Raven haired, refined, but cold.
I used to judge; now I'm spent,
And trespass where I can't repent.
Judge me, then: I pant, expire,
Brought to ground by cruel desire.

**Notes:** Dyddgu, the dark-haired lady who divided Dafydd's affections after his encounter with the golden-haired Morfudd, may well have been a real person, but the names of her father and grandfather are too common for her to be identified conclusively with a historical figure. The opening of the poem, with its flattery of Dyddgu's father for his warlike valour and his generosity, is highly conventional and unrealistic for the fourteenth century, but given the more self-ironic tone of the rest of the poem, and its frank admission that Dyddgu is not interested, it seems likely that this poetic epistle was not really meant for the eyes of a prospective father-in-law. The long penultimate stanza of the poem – a masterpiece in the original, with its marvellously elongated opening sentence – is an extended reference to the story of 'Peredur Son of Efrog' in the *Mabinogion*. In the *Mabinogion* version, a hawk has killed a duck in the snow, and a raven comes to eat the flesh, but Peredur, viewing the scene of carnage, sees instead the face of the beloved: the blackness of the raven is the woman's hair, the whiteness of the snow is her face, and two spreading stains of blood in the snow are the two red spots in her cheeks. In Dafydd's version, the raven has disappeared, and the duck is replaced by a blackbird or ouzel. By poetic convention, a beautiful woman's hair was often compared with the plumage of the blackbird. The Magi mentioned in the previous stanza are unlikely to be the visitors at the Nativity: they are almost certainly the wise men who interpreted the dream of the Emperor Maxen in the tale of *Breuddwyd Maxen*.

## *Under the Eaves*
Dan y Bargod

Listen, girl – I am locked out
And sick for love, torn by doubt –
Show yourself and sulk no more,
Dour behind your bolted door.
By Mair! I'll gnash teeth and wail
Should your falsity prevail!

Clammed with cold, three times I tapped
(Your knocker broke); I listened rapt
For your footfalls. I'm fearing
That my girl's hard of hearing.
Morfudd! Open now in haste!
No use claiming to be chaste!
Warm within? I quake without.
Are you deaf! Why, then I'll shout!
A windy night brings ruin, wrack:
Pity this insomniac!
Have a heart! Grim is my plight!
Wind howls in wrath tonight,
Torrents cascade from the eaves.
My yearning flesh – how it grieves –
Now there's sleet, the air frigid
Blows on me, frozen rigid.
It's not that I'm soft or nesh –
Merely made of mortal flesh.
I watch – you left me in the lurch –
There never was a colder perch
Than this: it's less dank and wet
In Caernarfon's oubliette!

I would not endure this gale
For any joy but your pale
Alluring form – nor the rain –
Only you are worth the pain,
And I alone have such love
To bear the elements above,
For only I assay your worth:
A glimpse of you costs the earth.

While I tremble in this mire,
In your slippers by the fire
You sit within. A wraith is all
That awaits without your wall:
My true soul has come inside.

It's wondrous that I haven't died
With waiting. I live, I cope,
By mortgaging my one hope:

Where are you? I plead and kneel.
Lift the latch: we made a deal!

**Notes:** Rachel Bromwich has suggested that this poem is an early Welsh appropriation of the *serenade* genre, appropriated from 13th century Spanish and Italian poems. If so, then the self-irony so evident throughout the poem is compounded by its Welsh setting: serenades may have been songs of loving complaint, but they were intended to be performed in a Mediterranean climate. The reference to Caernarfon castle may have carried specific contemporary reference: it is possible that some well known Welsh personality was languishing in the dungeon there, since the fortress was an imposing bastion of English rule. The poem is, of course, a blatant attempt to win the affections of a married woman, and thus also draws on earlier troubadour traditions, but this is not to say that the situation is entirely fictitious. There are hints in some of Dafydd's other poems that Morfudd was beaten by her husband Eiddig.

# *Fighting for Morfudd*
Achub Gwraig Eiddig

Girl who obscures her white throat
Pale and blenched – Eiddig's threat
Hangs over you, a sick blight:
You it is he'll beat tonight.
In rude health and humour ill,
No one can predict his will.
He scorns to play at love, girl,
All his life the vilest churl,
Hating hope, forsaking love –
May he spurn heaven above!
His own sister risks his ire
To speak with you. Hellish fire
Forbids the prude to permit
Discourse with a holy hermit
Lest it sully you. By night
He won't let you out of sight,
Yet you elude the fool by day:
Contrive to have things your way.

I myself have risked my life
In dalliance with Eiddig's wife:
Then he thrashed you. Catch your breath
And wish the ogre sudden death
Who dares to judge you. Hear now,
Gleaming one with golden brow:
Two things I would do – take note –
Were I in your petticoat.
Divorce the brute while you can;
Marry with a gentler man.
Death! Come lurk beside the bed
Where the bruiser lays his head!
I would not weep to see his corpse
Ride to earth the wooden horse
Shrouded like a wormy ghost.
Come to him who loves you most.

**Notes:** Three of the eleven manuscripts attribute it to Dafydd, and in the rest it is left anonymous, but Thomas Parry, the mid-twentieth century editor of his poems, thought it too 'unrefined' to be the work of the master. I have endeavoured to retain an air of coarseness through some metrical inconsistencies, but I suspect the poem is Dafydd's work, and that the rough and ready tone is a symptom of genuine anger. Although Morfudd is not mentioned in the text, I have chosen the title in preference to 'Rescuing Eiddig's Wife' because the name Eiddig is consistently used by Dafydd when referring to the husband of his golden girl. There is another poem, 'Llychwino Pryd y Ferch', which Parry does accept as Dafydd's work, in which the poet laments the fact that Morfudd's beauty has faded because of ill treatment at the hands of her husband. The phrase

"Were I in your petticoat" is a more or less literal translation of an idiomatic phrase akin to the English "Were I in your shoes". The wooden horse is, of course, a coffin, so the poem can be read as a magical satire against Eiddig, but there is also a possibility that the line contains an allusion to the old Welsh custom of Ceffyl Pren, in which an abusive marriage partner was publicly humiliated on a wooden horse. Since the participants in this ritual were often cross-dressed, it is possible that the reference to the "petticoat" in an earlier line is also a punning allusion to the practice (Huw Davies, *pers. comm.*, 2009.)

# *Love Pangs*
Poen Serch

Your sleek shape and symmetry
Rob my sleep and sanity:
Pale I am to look upon,
Lost for words and woebegone.
Must you keep me here to brood
On your empty platitudes,
Little fibs? I fret and frown,
Doubt, desire, and fall down.
You flatter me, in your keeping
Like a caged thing, cold, weeping,

My tongue dumb, deprived of skill,
Stuttering to please your will.
Kill me outright if you can –
Better than deprive a man
Of sanity. Girl, you mock
And make me reel with sick shock.
White as chalk, your chiselled face
Saps my colour, sucks the grace
From words whispered to my jewel:
Soft she shines but ever cruel.
Girl who grieves beside my bed,
Your love-curse will leave me dead.

A lark I am, snared in lime,
Struggling to escape the slime,
Adhering more each flutter:
Every faking word you utter
Transfixes me, saps my luck,
Leaves me smeared, entwined and stuck
To the twig, piteous sight,
The more I aspire to flight.

The fool climbs, and thinks him free
The higher he ascends the tree
Closer to the leafy crown:
He has further to fall down.
I am the outlaw, once bold,
Bound to swing from some scaffold,
Languishing inside a cell
Awaiting sentence: bliss or hell.
I am a lamb: bleating shape
Behind a wolf with no escape,
Following with trust too blind

To plumb the deceiver's mind.
Lost to love, my ardour bounds
Like Maelgwn's staglorn hounds.

Before early morning light
Dafydd shall be killed outright.
You think I jest, Golden One?
Love lies dead and I am gone.

**Notes:** All three manuscripts of this poem are anonymous, but it is in Dafydd's style. Close similarities between some lines of this poem and others of contemporary style may suggest that this is a pastiche, but it is certainly not incompatible with the overall picture of the rise and decline of Dafydd's love for Morfudd. The poem follows literary convention by listing a string of metaphors – some more extended than others – for the sufferings of a lover. The most striking of these refers to the barbaric practice of smearing twigs with 'lime' derived from mistletoe berries in order to trap songbirds by gluing them to the bark. The more a bird struggles when trapped in lime, the more its feet and feathers are entangled. Bird-liming appears to have been quite common in the mediaeval period when wild birds – even ones as small as larks – were a freely available source of protein, and unfortunately, it is one of those "traditions" that continues to this day, albeit more covertly. Maelgwn Gwynedd was a 6th century king of Gwynedd, and there appears to have been an oral tradition involving his hounds.

# *The Melody*
Y Gainc

My muse gave me melody
Where I sang mock-merrily:
A man who plucks his hope
On the taut strings of his harp.
Here on my bench, I'm testing
The tune I learned by trysting,
Weaving words for my old flame:
Warp and weft on love's loom.

Yet all girls in the region
Scorn my amorous raging –
More fool me, that I played it –
"A simpleton has made it!"

I sang with a guileless art
A psalm to pluck her heart:
Lovely melody of mine,
Much approved by all young men,
A minstrel's skilful praise
To the envy of my peers,
A birdsong – pride of poets –
A plaint that won applause.

Alas, though love endear it,
That Dyddgu cannot hear it.
Let her heed, if she's alive,
My nightingale song of love!
The high string of Hildr's skill
On a drunk, ascending scale,
Like splendid English psaltery.
No French piper, slavishly
Complaining of his malady,
Ever matched my melody:

Freeze his lips, O winter,
And may his fingers wither!
But God will lend his help
To this hopeful, and his harp,
Who for his gold-girl madly
Sings this fool's glad melody.

**Notes:** The cywydd was a verse form designed to be recited or sung to a harp accompaniment, and there can be little doubt that Dafydd was a proficient instrumentalist and composer. In Dafydd's words, the harp is literally "love's embroidering frame", but for reasons of metrics and consonance, I have interpreted this as "love's loom". It is not entirely clear who is the intended victim of the satire in the last verse: I have chosen to make the French piper the object of Dafydd's scorn, but it is possible that he meant to leave his curse on any rival bard choosing to hijack Dafydd's poem for amorous purposes of his own. Dyddgu is the name of one of Dafydd's two most enduring love-interests. Hildr is more problematic. It is a Norse name, used in the Edda for one of the Valkyries. It is likely, however, that Dafydd is employing it as a stock name for a master-harper, just as names such as Eigr are used in other poems as types of beautiful women. For an excellent exploration of the possible sources of the name Hildr in this poem, see: Sally Harper, 'Dafydd ap Gwilym: Poet and Musician', at www.dafyddapgwilym.net.

## *Her False Oath*
Llw Gau

Wanton girl who beamed and lied
With casual oath, and denied
Our dalliance on the Cross,
Spurned my favours – to her loss –
And claimed – peril on her soul –
My naked limb did not steal
Her eager touch! Though she be loth
Enid must take back her oath!

Yes, yes, poet's hand *did* grip
That poet's gift. Yes, the lip!
Yes, breasts, beneath birchy wood,
Yes, arms! Behold – it was good –
Yes, every quaking member,
Yes, wantonness! Remember?
A barefaced liar, beggar you!
God knows! There's nought we *didn't* do!

**Notes:** One of Dafydd's shortest poems, and one of a handful which are more or less sexually explicit. Enid is not the girl's name, but a conventional title for a woman of exceptional beauty.

## *That Near-Nun from Eithinfynydd*
Y Fun o Eithinfynydd

In Eithinfynydd – sore test –
A girl lives who scorns to tryst.
Fine of eyebrow, warm of glance,
Fair of hair, she frowns askance.
Fatal muse – fettered my breath,
Fortified from fear of death –
Flaming mirror, glazed in gold,
Fire-lit jewel who thrills the glade,
For me she was forged, her grace
Flintlike as her ivory face.
Forgoing lust, my lithe love
Forswears trysting in the grove.
Never ventures to the woods
Nor answers amorous words.
No, my Morfudd will not play,
Not for love of Mair, but pray,
Loving only saints, and Christ –
No faith in me – she is chaste.
Nothing she knows of my state –
Never would she fornicate –
Not knowing I would be true,
Not wanting me, nor him, nor you.
Never would I wish to live
Forfeiting my heartfelt love,
So I suffer pain and dearth:
To flirt with Morfudd means death.

**Notes:** A farm between Llanuwchllyn and Dolgellau, Meirionethshire, goes by the name of Eithinfynydd, but this is also the name for a dwelling near Tal-y-bont. The idea that Morfudd's refusal is prompted by her religious devotion appears in some of Dafydd's other poems, and it is perhaps significant that he first met her at the performance of a mystery play. However, other poems make it clear that she was married to an abusive husband. Perhaps the two scenarios are not mutually exclusive. Thomas Parry included the poem in his 1952 edition of Dafydd's work, but questioned its authenticity. Later critics have been more confident, citing independent sources which connect Morfudd with Meirionethshire. If the poem is not by Dafydd ap Gwilym, it is a very good imitation by one of his near-contemporaries. Based on the text available at www.dafyddapgwilym.net.

## *Nun-Baiting*
Cyrchu Lleian

Loyal *llatai*, be at peace:
March yields to May at a pace.

Now, by God, I need again
Your services. I have grown
Desperate. The place? You know!
You did well there last time. Go!

Get to the nunnery, bird,
Where you got girls once before
For Dafydd. Tell the gaoler
I've psalms to gild her glamour:
Pitch my line before the Nones,
Sing my praise, and get me nuns!
Fly into their cells, pour
*Cywydd* in their ears. They're pure
As gossamer spilt with snow,
And that is why I want them so.
Each one is a swallow white:
Morfudd's sisters, plumed for flight.

Your two feet are perfect tools
For plying girls from choirs. Rules
Are for novices only.
Bring to the grove a black-robed
Nun, stolen beneath the nose
Of the Frater: she's a rose
From his garden. Sixty others
He can keep, and call Mothers
Inferior. I know! Get
The Chantress. She's like snow: wet,
White, enticing. No? I guess
You'll have to bring the Abbess.

**Notes:** This is a llatai (love messenger) poem with a difference, for here the carrier of Dafydd's message is not identified, although it is almost certainly a bird, given that it has only two legs, and needs to be nimble enough to infiltrate a nunnery. The original text specifies the place: the Cistercian foundation at Llanllugan on the Welsh Marches, which would undoubtedly have been a particularly difficult stronghold to breach in amorous terms, given that the founder of these monasteries, St Bernard of Clairvaux, would have been more horrified than many of his contemporaries by the dalliances the poet proposes. Although Dafydd is apparently prepared to receive any of the nuns in his woodland grove, it is likely that the Abbess is the real objective all along, for she is certainly the gaoler of line 12. Lines 24-25, with their somewhat subversive gloss on the Rule of St. Benedict, are my own invention, but I maintain that they are not out of keeping with Dafydd's intention. Dafydd's authorship of this scurrilous poem is not contested, although it is certain that it spawned a bastard progeny of imitations, some of which may in fact have been variations on the theme, written by the master himself. See, for example, the possibly apocryphal – and more likely authentic - 'Loving a Nun' (Caru Lleian). It is worth noting that the poem is not a complete betrayal of loyalty: the proposed nun-conquests are only placebos for Dafydd's true beloved: the infinitely beautiful, and inconveniently married Morfudd. He may have been a sexual predator, but at least he was one with a sense of humour.

## *The Greeting Unspoken*
Yr Annerch

Welcome – don't welcome – envoy,
The wife I don't know. Convey
My covert greeting. Entreat
Her obliquely (I fear some threat):
"Come quickly". I don't know who
She is. I'll meet her – nowhere.
As for me, I shall arrive
Whenever I cease to rove.
Should she ask, "Who's the suitor?"
(No question sour or sweeter)
Say, refraining from all talk,
"I don't know." And should you take
A shut-eyed glance at her face,
Eclipsing, ghostlike, her fierce
Radiance, then you must both
Say nought, by your unsworn oath!

**Notes:** Although it is among the shortest, it is also one of the most untranslatable of Dafydd's poems, with its string of oxymorons interrupted by parentheses. The reason for this confusing structure is – again paradoxically - quite clear: Dafydd wishes to meet his beloved, but he is afraid to arrange a time or a venue for fear of reprisals from her husband, and afraid even to ask his messenger to say anything to her at all.

## *The Nocturnal Lovers Part at Dawn*
Y Wawr

It was a long night. I set
At nought all other nights. Sweet
Dalliance we had. I sigh
To think how its rival nights
Fall short. Surely a whole week
Was in it – yet 'twas fast work.

Last night, I could scarce handle
Nia, dark heaven's candle.
I gave respect, expecting
Some reward for prospecting
With such high optimism.
My grip was like a prison-
Lock, and yet, I swear, she yawned
And proclaimed that it was dawn.

"Get up!" she chirped, "It's the sun
Which lights my robe, a bright sign
Of waking. No more weeping,
Bad boy – go, while they're sleeping!"

*He:* Soft, slender, scheming maiden,
I've a hunch you're mistaken:
It's the moon - a gift from God -
And stars. I can get a good
Look at you at last. Don't drone
On, insisting it's the dawn!"

*She:* If we're safe beneath night's cloak,
Why can I hear raven croaks?

*He:* Some old rat must gnaw the root
Of the tree where ravens roost.

*She:* If dawn's not near, why the bark
Of dogs in the not-quite dark?

He: Hold me close – no need for fright –
You're safe from the Hounds of Night!

She: Daft poet! No more ruses!
I'm done with wild excuses –
Off you go. Mope not! I'd say
You've more amours planned when day
Breaks anyway. Please make sure

You're quiet opening the door.
Run for the woods, ere the hounds
Chase you to ground, bound by bound.

*He:* The spinney with its sharp spears
Is a place the bloodhounds fear:
I'll hide there. Eiddig won't find
Me. I'm fleet as any hind.

*She:* Sweet poet! But I shall yearn!
Swear to God that you'll return!

*He:* Till the night when darkness fails,
Girl, I'll be your nightingale.

**Notes:** The theme of the parting of lovers at dawn was a favourite one in French poetry, and found its way into English in the parting scene between Romeo and Juliet on the morning after their marriage, and from there into John Donne's 'The Sun Rising' – but it found its way into Welsh two centuries before Shakespeare. Of course, Dafydd's poem does not take the theme entirely seriously. The "Hounds of Night" are the hounds of the Wild Hunt: spectral beasts loyal to Gwyn ap Nudd, who also play a role in the First Branch of the *Mabinogion.* Nia, or Nyf, is the Irish heroine of the Ossian cycle, Oisín's beloved, but is also the Welsh word for 'snow'. In this context, it is clearly a stock name for a desirable woman, since white skin and dark brows were traditional signs of beauty.

# Love-messengers

## *The Song Thrush*
Y Ceiliog Bronfraith

I heard the loving cock thrush long
Pour out pure and limpid song
In brightest diction, beneath the birch,
As fine as any voice in church,
Diminutively whistling clear.
No sweeter song could charm the ear.

He reads a matins, leaves me blest,
His chasuble his feathered breast.
From the thicket where he takes his stand
His voice rings out across the land.
Hillside prophet, longing's pope,
Impassioned poet of wooded slope,
In cadence clear within the vale
He sings his word of passion. Hale
And happy lyrics from him spill:
Quavers, crotchets from his bill,
All to please a girl who waits
And love's conundrums soft debates.
The air his lectionary, he a preacher
Pure and sweet, inspired teacher,
Flawless, following Ovid's way,
Gentle bishop of bright May.

I know him. At the birchwood tryst
He it is who sings the list
Of love's birds, chorusing in the glade
Their odes, in dappled light and shade.
He seeks the hazel, there to sing
Within the copse, on angel's wing.
In Paradise, the songsters cease,
Incline their heads to hear his piece,
And god can find no holy bird
Who dares recall each note and word.

**Notes:** Dafydd distinguished between the Song Thrush and the Mistle Thrush, and wrote poems about both.

# *The Roebuck*
Y Carw

Hurry, Roebuck, antlered fugitive,
Grey fetlocked, swift, furtive,
With great haste, take my letter,
On your backside, to my lover.
Fast loper, furlong leaper,
Most willing love-bearer,
Carry it, Roebuck, spurred by god,
To Dyddgu, girl of aspect glad.

He grazes grass in his lair of ling
Beyond the carn, with antlers long
Dealing fairly with the poet,
Wild-headed, leaping the height –
Bare of bottom, like a lamb,
Fair of face, and lithe of limb.
Fine-headed baron, fear no betrayal,
My hearty lad no hound dare slay.
With lissom feet: a worthy feat
Than hunting hounds to be more fleet.
Have no fear of dogs who lope,
Nor lethal arrows, if you can leap.
Look out for Pali, brown of foot,
And Iolyth, fast and fleet,
Pay wary heed to hound and horse
Until you come to Dyddgu's house.
Keep out of clearings, lest you're broken,
Climb the hill, hide in the bracken,
Dodge the hedge, dip through the field,
Delay no more, or hope has fled.

Trusted messenger, faithful deer,
Take my poem to Dyddgu's door.
Hurry now! Trot forth with courage!
I hear her father keeps her caged.
Fear not his anger. Fast be gone
And make more haste than Actaeon!
At night, beneath the trees come back
And look for me beside the bank;
Bring me her kiss – I'll make no complaint –
From a fair coloured girl, hair in a plait.
Excellent Roebuck! Sally forth!
None shall flay you – keep your faith!
You go where I fear to be caught –
No English churl shall wear your coat –
No, darling! Nor the cuckold brash

Have horns or hooves, or your dear flesh.

You will survive (if god be wise),
All treachery. Cynfelyn's curse
On your foe. I too bless
You, who bear the rosehip's blush.

**Notes:** The line "Make more haste than Actaeon is literally "impelled by understanding of Ovid's ways" (Bromwich). I have elected to make Dafydd's reference more explicit: Ovid's Actaeon was killed by his own hounds after he was transformed into a stag. Dafydd emulated Ovid as a poet; perhaps he also admired his Pythagorean reverence for nature. Dafydd has his own word for the potentially jilted husband or cuckold: *Eiddig*. He may well have intended the joke implied in the next line, in which the prospective cuckold is deprived of his horns. Saint Cynfelyn, patron saint of the church of Llangynfelyn. In the original, this stanza is a prayer for the roebuck's protection, but the idea of Dafydd invoking a curse from the saint seems no more incongruous than the idea that a saint would be interested in the first place, given that Dafydd's love is adulterous.

## *The Seagull*
Yr Wylan

Seagull, floating with the flow,
Coloured like the moon, or snow,
Gleaming where the dark tides run,
Upon the wave a shard of sun,
A glint of light, proud and pure
Pursuing fish through seas azure,
A gleam at anchor, chained but free,
Kedged to lilies of the sea:

My girl, most ripe for praise, espy.
Around her rocks and ramparts fly
To catch a glimpse of Eigr's form .
Let your eye her fortress storm.
Tell her it is she I need –
Let her choose me, slake my greed –
And if she is alone, then greet
Her, dripping at her lissom feet.
Be skilful: my advantage gain.
I win her, or I die in pain.

I love her. I'm compelled by lust.
No man who lived and turned to dust
Loved more, charmed by Myrddin's spell.
Taliesin could not tell
Of fairer form: her copper tresses,
The body Aphrodite blesses .
Seagull, seagull! Fly and seek
The sunset gleaming in her cheek.
Let loving words be on her breath
Or else I meet untimely death.

**Notes:** According to *Brut y Brenhinedd*, Eigr was the mother of Arthur (Ygraine), a most beautiful woman who is consistently praised by Dafydd as the archetype of feminine form. The *Cynfeirdd* Taliesin and Merlin are invariably coupled together as poets with the gift of prophecy, especially in later Arthurian tradition. They are traditionally believed to have lived in the sixth century. Anthony Conran makes an ingenious suggestion that Dafydd is making an alchemical pun with his reference to Aphrodite. Dafydd's word "Sipris" is normally translated "Venus", since she was the Cyprian, whose alchemical metal was copper.

## *The Greenwood Mass*
Offeren y Llwyn

Happy among hazel's mantles,
Shadowed by green marvels
I listened at rise of sun
As a thrush improvised a song:
An englyn of great mastery ,
With joy's lessons and mysteries.

Wise in nature; bird stranger
Come from far; grey messenger
From Camarthen, welcome guest
At my golden girl's request ,
His happy words a verbal volley
Lilting as he flew the valley.
Morfudd gave him commission,
May's fledgeling, poet of passion.
His cassock was his coat of feathers,
Coped in hawthorn, happy Father.
His stole, in which he spoke his Word,
Was the winged green seeds of wind .

I could swear by great god
The chancel roof was wrought in gold,
The chanting clear, the language loud
Without a pause: hear the Lord.
In syllables that could not perish
He read his gospel to his parish;
A round leaf on an earthen sod
He consecrated unto god .
Philomel, elegant, slender,
Within the thicket was his server:
A poetess who flew, and rang
The Sanctus bell, and purely sang
And lifted up the holy host
To the heavens above the copse –
Ecstasy in her cup of gold –
And brightly pledged her love to god.

I'm well pleased with what I've fathered:
A psalm the sacred birchwood fostered.

**Notes:** The *englyn* was a traditional verse form, already ancient in Dafydd's day, which was well adapted to religious themes, as he demonstrated himself in his '*Englynion Yr Offeren*'. When he mentions that the bird has come by his "golden girl's request", Dafydd innovates to stretch the boundaries of a convention he has himself created: the *llatai*, or love messenger, in this poem, is the thrush, but Dafydd does not send him to Morfudd: the bird is an emissary from the girl. This is the first of many surprises in this adventurous poem. The bird's stole, in Bromwich's translation, is the "winged green mantles of the wind", suggests the winged seeds of the ash or sycamore; I have endeavoured to make this reading explicit. The consecration of the leaf is the poem's second innovation: not only is the thrush personified as a priest performing the Mass; a round leaf becomes the consecrated wafer. Readers alone can judge whether Dafydd here crosses the line from orthodox spiritual enthusiasm into more delectable heresy, especially given that the bird is also a message-bearer from a married woman.

## *The Titmouse*
Y Ceiliog Coed

Swift, timorous tot of a bird,
Bell-voiced titmouse: fly beyond –
Far south, to where the sun shimmers –
Fair is she who gives her summons.
Feiriawn's englyn: I find no fault,
Recited from brambles, bright in the field.
From branching birches, sing lovelorn laments
My little squire of the white helmet.

Plaintive, gentle, bird of calmness,
Blessed with plumage of four colours:
Bright blue; sap green, gleaned from leaves;
White and black from the moods of lovers.
Diminutive bard of youth's ardour,
My tiny knight in downy armour,
Package of mystery, cheeky sprite,
Carry my secret, spry and swift:

The wind lead you to Meirionnydd,
Fur-clad wife of wry Dafydd,
My golden girl of gaze beguiling –
Go swiftly, and give her greeting.
She is the mistress I may not mention
To any man. Beseech her, call her maiden,
Say anything! Insist she wait,
Withhold from him her flesh as white
As sea-foam! The soul within me fades!
See that memory of me fails
Not a moment. Lively, honoured
Titmouse, by the hawk unharmed,
Slim-footed, gentle-feathered,
By the fervent woodland fathered,
Pert persuader, work your wings
Above the trees, in gloom and winds;
Reveal my purpose, and make plain
That she alone has caused my pain.
Woodland magus, diligent poet,
Pledge my troth and take my part,
Say I am banished beyond the border,
Compelled to bide here with my brother.
Seven cares constrict my heart,
An archer's shaft compounds my hurt.
A whole month, bright-voiced bird,
Have I yearned for Dafydd's bride,
And though she pledges me her love

It is a miracle I live.

**Notes:** A more likely author than Dafydd was Llywelyn Goch ap Meurig Hen; it seems a mere coincidence that the poet's love-rival was also named Dafydd. Helen Fulton (Dafydd ap Gwilym, Apocrypha, Dyfed, 1996) translates "penloyn" as "coal-tit", but I have gone for the more generic "titmouse", since of the poet's description of the bird's colouration more closely matches that of the blue-tit or great-tit. The latter are certainly commoner birds. "Penloyn" is derived from "pen" (head) and "gloyn" (piece of coal), a description which matches no bird in particular. From a paraphraser's perspective, the poem presents certain difficulties: it is more conventional than Dafydd's verse, and somewhat repetitious. There is a marked contrast between the jewel-like freshness of the poet's address to the bird, and his rather maudlin musings on Meirionnydd; I have tried to even these out as much as possible, but it is difficult to avoid a weak ending. I fear I have not entirely avoided a reference to Burns in the opening couplet.

# The Trout
Y Brithyll

Swimmer in praise, gleaming trout,
Bright of discourse, fast as thought,
Fearless fish, feeding aflow,
Currents above, deeps below,
Swirling foundling, foster fish
Of Llyn Tegid, full of flesh,
Swim the Conwy, scry the stream,
Seek the highland, scales agleam.

None but you, water-father,
Serves me still: out of favour,
Exiled, spurned, sent from sight.
Swim the Tâf's wave of light,
Valiant, immune to steel,
Undrownable, never still,
Speechless, breathless current-wender,
Cryptic shadow under water.
You do not need, by great God
To fear fly or willow rod.
Poet's stalwart, spawn of Môn,
Flowing river's talisman,
Torrent-fish of flux and flood,
Foam-rider, staunch of blood,
Ransom of the landing net,
Glimpsed by campers in the wet,
Twist and slither, snap two snares,
Short and sleek, free from cares,
Go by grace, be not taken.
For my heart, take this token:
A loving pledge – lithe fish, slender –
May I give the slip to slander!

To Creirwy's court, by my whim,
Go forthwith, then cease to swim.
Handless go, as to heaven;
Footless, return to haven.
Linger not by ford nor burn;
Bring fishy tales when you return.

**Notes:** Most of the fourteen manuscripts of this poem attribute it to Dafydd; the remainder do not name a poet. Recent scholars have questioned Dafydd's authorship, and although none of the manuscripts name him, Gruffudd Gryg (writing c. 1357-70) has been suggested. Llyn Tegid is Bala Lake, Meirionnydd, north-west Wales. Conwy is the name of a river as well as a town. The river Tâf flows southwards through Carmarthenshire, emptying into the sea at Laugharne. 'The Trout' is a traditional llatai poem in which a non-human agency is called upon to act as a love messenger. The poet's beloved, Creirwy, is also traditional: a beauty whose name appears in Hanes Taliesin and in the Triads. I have taken certain liberties with meaning in order to preserve some of the tone and rhythm of the original. In particular, I have reversed the meaning of the phrase "croyw awdur o Fôn" (founder of Môn), since the meaning is rather obscure, and "spawn of Môn" seems to suit a fish. For metrical reasons I have also left out a phrase, "Deifr ni'th feiddian", translated by Fulton: "the men of Deira cannot defy you", which in context probably means that the trout is immune to attacks from the English.

## *A Dream from Annwn*
Y Breuddwyd

Within my grove once I stole,
Courting sleep profound and still.
Day began to squint and yawn,
A dream upon the brow of morn.
*Greyhounds loping at my side*
*Stalking down a woodland ride,*
*I saw a mansion, no mean hut,*
*Unleashed my hounds, let them hunt,*
*And through the wood, echoed sounds:*
*Hot for blood, my baying hounds.*

*Flushed with chasing, soon I saw*
*A white doe dash the forest floor;*
*On her trail, in hot pursuit,*
*My hounds – I followed in a sweat –*
*She shot across a wooded ridge,*
*Along two spurs. With lusty rage*
*My hounds chased her back again,*
*Stag-swift, snapping in her train,*
*When at once she turned, and came*
*As if for mercy, quaking, tame.*
*Her naked nostrils brushed my arm*
- And I awoke, as by a charm.

A witch I sought, to say sooth
- For I was thirsty now for truth –
Bidding her, by second sight
Explain the portents of the night:
"Wise woman, spin your spell,
Unwind my wyrd, by God or Hell,
Search my soul, read my dream,
And I shall hold you in esteem."

"Man, forsooth, it augurs well.
Raise your hopes, awake your will:
The hounds revelling in the hunt
Who hurtled on and would not halt
Are *llateion*, and their zest
Surely aids your ardent quest.
The doe's the lady that your heart
Pursues for love, alive with heat.

She shall come. Unclench your fist.
God prepare you for the tryst."

**Notes:** It is clear from other poems that the fourteenth century bard was well-versed in the tales of the *Mabinogion*, and it is difficult to avoid a suggestion of their influence here. Perhaps the narrator is Pwyll, a one-time visitor to Annwn, and no stranger to the supernatural hunt. Perhaps the lady is Rhiannon, who eluded Pwyll and his men when they gave chase, but turned and sought his hand in marriage when he called for her. In this poem, the magical context is overt: the dreamer seeks the advice of a wise-woman: a fortune teller who can read his dream, and her response makes it clear that the *llatai* convention was more than just a poetic device. The *llatai*, or love-messenger, nearly always took the form of a mammal or bird, or occasionally an elemental force, and in the context of the present poem, the *llatai* hounds seem to represent the poet's own fetch, sent out in his sleep to seek his beloved. There is a further parallel to the 'Dream of Maxen' in the *Mabinogion*, which also combines a hunting scene with a dreaming vision of a beloved woman, but the idea that the dream must be interpreted by a woman with magical powers is at least as old as Ovid. Even here, however, Dafydd achieves a realism that defies convention and suggests personal experience: note, for example, the fact that the sleeper is awoken as soon as he is touched by the nostrils of the doe. At the end of the poem, I have chosen to highlight a further mediaeval convention: the rather disturbing metaphor which compares the entrapment of a desired woman to the driving of a deer towards a trysting tree, where a lord or king lurks in wait for the kill. See, for example, Chaucer's *Troilus and Criseyde*, lines 1527-1535.

## *The Salmon*
Yr Eog

Sea-sleek salmon, you have gained
Every blessing under God,
By Mair, bright, unlimited,
Finely delineated,
Haughty underwater bird,
Hawk of eddies, slick-scaled bard,
Swift, yet footless underneath.
The portcullis of your teeth
Snaps on sand-eels, spectral form,
Fish of gravel and white foam.

I will make, by art, charm or
Stanzas, a suit of armour
Against bag-nets, Eigr's moon,
Against trawling, against weir-men,
Against gutting, against hooks,
Against the brutal man who hacks
From his coracle, hard upon
Your bronze scales; against harpoons.

Since I'd hear your tale, all perils
Evade, navigating ripples
Undaunted. Ride the ocean swell
'Til you reach uncharted soil:
Two tall river banks, a lake,
And last, where the waters lick
Land in moonlight, a linnet
Unrolled, like a length of linen
Upon the surface: watch her,
Call her, glass-eyed fly-catcher,
Woo away from Eiddig's bed
My white-faced girl, black browed,
Arm fair as moonlit cloud,
Each breast a sun, her skin: flour,
Wearing a gold ring, I fear.

I ail! Unedifying
It is to see! On finding
Her, golden-crowned linnet,

Ask twice my second Luned:
Leap before her breast and greet
Her like a fountain. Like great
Modred tell her straight, that flake
Of snow, moon above the lake:

My heart is dead from wanting;
My breast is speared with waiting.
Fair, courtly girl, near the grave
I am. Yet, if in this grove
You should stoop to strip four leaves
From the cuckoo's twigs - by love's
Luck – then, quarter them, and throw
Them in the water, the flow
Will carry them fast to me,
Afloat upon the estuary.
I'll fish, though she betrayed me,
Let not one leaf evade me.

**Notes:** Perhaps Dafydd's most difficult and most rewarding poem, this stretches the *llatai* convention to its limits whilst indulging in an exquisitely complex wordplay which entwines Celtic mythology with the poem's own surreal aesthetic. Luned (Lynette in the French romances) was the handmaiden of the Lady of the Fountain in the *Mabinogion*: the selfless lover of Owain the knight. Dafydd stretches his puns to breaking point: his lover is a second Luned because of her beauty, but this is also the second time he has beseeched her for love, making this his second wish (*ail uned*), and her reflection on the surface of the lake (*llyn*) takes for a moment the form of a linnet (*llinos*), and then the form of a length of linen (*llin*) or flax, from a Cheapside shop. The word *linnet* is derived from the Old English *linece*, and before it, the Latin *linum*, both words for flax, because linnets were thought to rely on flax seeds (linseeds) for their staple diet. In the interests of preserving this complex display of linguistic wit, I have departed entirely from the literal meaning of lines 35-6, cramming it into later lines, in order to retain the letter sequence "ail uned" in English: a trick I hope Dafydd would have appreciated. I have also taken the liberty of including some *lunar* references. Dafydd asserts that the salmon is the most perfect sea creature God has created (*a luniwyd*), and in modern Welsh, *lluniwr* is the former or maker. Thus, my version of Dafydd's salmon is "finely delineated". A further reference to 'The Lady of the Fountain' may be hidden in line 8, "*Fal bars yn dy fol y bwyd*" ("food like bars in your belly" – *bars* is a word borrowed from English). Helen Fulton suggests that this is a reference to the salmon's habit of devouring long, thin, silvery sand-eels, but of course, the other creature with bars in its belly is Sir Owain's horse, which was sliced in two by the portcullis of his enemy's castle as he chased his foe beneath it. Modred (or Mordred) was not maligned as Arthur's enemy in Dafydd's day, but vaunted as a great storyteller, and presumably, a great persuader. Suffice to say, Dafydd's lover is already married – hence the reference to the ring – and the twigs belong to her husband Eiddig, presumably because they are on his land. They are therefore the cuckoo's twigs, since Eiddig is a cuckold – or at least he will be if Dafydd has any say in the matter. It is likely that there are even deeper folkloric references in the poem. The choice of a salmon as *llatai* or love-messenger may well be influenced by Celtic legends which assert that a salmon became the repository of all wisdom by swallowing a hazel-nut. In some folk-tales, a man catches the salmon, fries it, burns his finger on it, and the moment he sucks away the heat, is instantly filled with all knowledge, like Gwion, who tasted the potion from Cerridwen's cauldron. As in the story of Gwion, there is more than a hint of shape-shifting in Dafydd's description of the girl's reflection on the water, as well as in his extraordinarily human salmon. It should be noted that this poem appears in radically different versions in other manuscripts.

## *The Swan*
Yr Alarch

Lake-swan, in lime-white habit,
Water-cloistered pale abbot,
My snowdrift-clean Cistercian
Bright as Transfiguration,
Puppet-headed swamp-preacher,
Arch-necked in plainsong-pleasure:
God gave you Llyn Yfaddon –
Deep as your neck can fathom –
And good gifts, at the Dawning,
To keep a swan from drowning.

King of fishers, thanks to luck,
Adrift upon the glazed lake,
You can fly to hills afar,
And no fowl has less to fear.
Remember, when you fly forth:
Scry the surface of the earth,
Plumb the depths where fish swim: slow,
Numerous as flakes of snow.
Fast work it is, wave-rider,
Water-glistered shoal-raider,
To catch a fish with fine flair –
Neck for rod and bill for lure.

Breast of foam, feathered snowflake,
Guard the secret of the lake.
Brook-ripples reflect your quills,
All agleam, as clear as quartz,
Clad in lilies. Haughty kings
Envy your unfurling wings.
Petal-feathered, wearing white
Meadow flowers that never wilt,
Cock of heaven, taunt of brides,
Envied by all other birds.

Turn your head to hearken, swan,
*Llatai* for a loving swain:
A girl lives close by your lees:
So coy. I am loth to lose
Her troth. My best-man swan, swim,

Questioning her woman's whim
With that looped neck. Seek my lover
At the oxbow downriver
From Tal-y-Llyn: coloured like
Mirrored moonlight in the lake.

Her name? Fear forbids my voice,
Therefore I encode in verse
Thus: after H, U, and then
Ds and Y to follow N.
Go web-footed to her bed;
Summon her with nodding head,
Sing my sorrow with your throat,
Tell her how each loving thought
Tortures me and makes me swoon:
Girl who dances like a swan.

God gave gifts that you might live;
I'll pay in grain, should she love.

**Notes:** There is no such lake as Llyn Yfaddon in Wales; it has been suggested that Dafydd means Llyn Syfaddon in Brycheiniog. There are several places called Tal-y-Llyn, but as these words mean "top of the lake", it is possible that this reference is merely descriptive. Whilst Dafydd's authorship has been contested, all twelve manuscripts attribute it to him, and it is very doubtful that the poem post-dates the mid-fifteenth century, since the girl's name is clearly Hunydd, which does not appear in genealogies after that date. Dafydd describes the swan as a "white abbot"; I have chosen to make it a Cistercian, since Dafydd is purportedly buried at Strata Florida Abbey, a Cistercian foundation. Dafydd's assumption that swans eat fish is erroneous: they subsist mainly on aquatic vegetation and invertebrates.

## *The Woodcock*
Y Ceiliog Coed

Woodcock, amongst hens adored,
Your black cloak with bronze adorned,
Brave bird with brow of coral,
Pica-pied, coped to carol,
Dappled bard: many a bride
Obeys you, young blueman-bird.
Castle-captain, girl-consoler,
Wood-cassocked self-concealer,
Kite-high outlaw, cloud-roding
Ghost abbot – call foreboding –
Dapper clergyman of oak
With your scapular of smoke,

Churchman in an autumn gown,
Friar hiding in the green,
Mottled livery, clad by winds
Your chasuble: folded wings,
Your doublet plumed wave-white,
Black-mantled, well-wrought.
Like a monk you dress, and live
Sworn to keep the Rule of Love,
Devout, dauntless, prayerful, bold,
Rain and birch your only bread
(A flock might feed on each branch
Of your holy hilltop birch).
Your work: twice a day, to call
Upon a host, that wild hens all
May have pleasure, flirt and swoon.
Such delight – but I presume!

You take part – by glade and leaf –
In dark obsequies of love.
Be my *llatai*, questing knight,
Take missives to my foam-white
Girl: go there on the morrow,
Dark-cloaked, eastwards – feign sorrow –
Until you fly by water-lees
And a vale of moonlit trees,
Where the river on the plain

Splits the meadowland in twain,
Where birds roost on harvest sheaves
And lapwings hide amid leaves.
Long billed *llatai*, there alight
At water's edge in dark night.
Watch, in woods where waters run,
And at the rising of the sun
Draw near to her, of Nyf's shade.
Fly, bird! Greet her in the glade –
For yesterday, she pledged troth
(I have a hunch she spoke truth)
And bade me love her, by the Pope!
So, it seems, I've grounds for hope.

Woodcock, hued by day and night,
My foam-white girl invite! Invite!
On yonder hill, she comes to me:
Lend your cloak, and none shall see.

**Notes:** It is possible that the poem is a fifteenth century imitation, but the detailed and observant description of the bird is typical of Dafydd's work. The poet makes much of the bird's particoloured plumage, which provides the living bird with such effective camouflage that when it stands still against a background of fallen leaves and withered bracken, it becomes virtually invisible. The solitary lifestyle of the bird, combined with its nocturnal habits and the male's habitual "roding" flights during courtship, make it an ideal choice for a *llatai*, or love messenger. The references to the magpie ("Pica-pied") and coral may seem odd in light of the brindled-brown colouration of the bird itself, but the poet doubtless makes these references – as well as implying that the bird is dressed in motley like a jester – as a means of describing the dappled appearance of the plumage. Five hundred years before Hopkins, Dafydd too saw glory in dappled things. The poet appears to think that the male woodcock has several mates, like a sultan with his harem; "blueman" is a literal translation of the Welsh "blowmon", which has previously been translated as "blackamoor". His conviction that the bird feeds only on water and birch-tips, whilst erroneous, is also doubtless based on observation. Woodcocks eat worms, but since they void their alimentary tracts whenever they take flight, birds which have been shot or captured always have empty stomachs. Because of this, the dietary preferences of woodcocks were still an enigma to Gilbert White in the eighteenth century, despite repeated dissection.

## *The Blackbird*
Y Ceiliog Mwyalch

Blackbird of judicious voice,
Even God never deceives
You, and your trim hymn rings true
Across the vale – regal, strong.
Nature's churchman, with no peer,
Bless your brow: your praise is pure.

Bird of greetings, fired with life,
Black-cassocked kindler of love,
Jesus clothes you, under leaves,
In black serge: the Tailor lines
Your cloak with satin, merry
As a rainbow – glistening murrey –
Caps you with a crest of silk
Weaved of summer, black and sleek,
Gives you a doublet, woven
Of Belgian wool, spun in bracken.
Out of jet he crafts your cheek;
Orange coral makes your beak.

Prophets praise you, call you bard –
Bird-baron, praised abroad –
Cantor of the green chorus,
Spindle-legged, nimble, careless,
Solicitous. You can reach
Any girl by tree and branch,
And in return, little swatch
Of verse, I'll sing praise, and vouch
That you are squire and scholar:
Pure black, yet every colour.
Harmony flows from your word;
Black your chasuble and hood.

Songsmith! Every poet knows
Mordred made no better noise!
God keep you pert and alive,
Beautiful-winged bird of love.

**Notes:** Although most of the ten surviving manuscripts of this poem attribute it to Dafydd ap Gwilym, it is quite likely that it is a fifteenth century imitation. If so, it is the work of a devoted disciple, who was clearly familiar with 'The Greenwood Mass', in which Dafydd personifies the birds as priests of the woodland in similarly daring terms. The "Belgian wool" ('blac-y-lir' in the original) is a reference to the woven woollen material originating from the town of Lire in Brabant. Murrey is a material, dark purple in colour, which was used in priestly vestments. Apart from being Arthur's enemy at the Battle of Camlann, Mordred was also renowned as a musician and poet.

## *Beseeching St. Dwynwen*
Galw ar Ddwynwen

Dwynwen, of frost's fragile form,
Enshrined in bright, waxen flame:
Your image, lit and gilded,
Is balm for hearts of jilted
Lovers. Men who keep vigils
Like Indeg's lorn evangels
Shall bear no sorrow within,
Nor carry sickness from Llanddwyn.

Your parish, in love's distress,
Is a flock of bleating strays,
And I, love's runt, am livid
From trailing my beloved
To no avail, my sick heart
Swollen with love's dropsy, hurt
By Morfudd. I may yet live,
But too coldly, shorn of love.

Heal me of the quaking hurt
Inflicting my feeble heart.
Goad God's grace to come alive,
Mediatrix of our love,
Gilt-spun saint, splashed with sun,
Who spurns gleaming snares of sin.
God cannot repent his wise
Welcome into Paradise
For Dwynwen. No prying prude
Will catch us conspiring. Crude,
Churlish Eiddig will not swat
Away my chaste patron saint.

No one will suspect that you,
Llanddwyn's virgin, would sneak to
Cwm-y-Gro on my behalf.
Your fair voice alone behoves
Men to obedience: all bend,
Pliant to your word. Your bard
And your God call you. Reveal
The kindness that your black veil
Conceals, and may God restrain
His groping hands with a chain:
That raping Eiddig whose bray
Echoes through the leaves of May
Pursuing us. Dwynwen, please,
Bring the girl who spurs my pulse

Beneath the trees of green May;
Touch my verse, and bless our play.
I prithee, pure Dwynwen: prove
Not every virgin's a prude.

Not because I pay pittance
At your shrine, but for penance
And prayers of yours – you who strove
Every hour you were alive
In devotion, and laid fresh
Chores each day on your fair flesh
In self-denial – for my sake,
Child of Brychan, pray, and seek
From Mair my deliverance –
Or blessing on our dalliance.

**Notes:** The cult of St. Dwynwen drew supplicants to the island of Llanddwyn, off the west coast of Anglesey, partly because of her reputation as a healer, but partly also because she was a patron saint of lovers. Dwynwen rejected her own "would be ravisher", as Rachel Bromwich puts it, and according to legend, he was turned to stone before she became a nun. It was claimed that she won a boon from God: any true lover who called upon her would either be requited, or be "healed" of the love itself. Dafydd pulls off a stupendously cheeky trick in this poem. As a saint, Dwynwen was regarded as a mediatrix between her supplicants and heaven, and whilst Dafydd half-appeals to her in this role, he also appropriates her as his *llatai* – his magical love-messenger – to mediate between Morfudd and himself. As a virginal saint, he surmises, she is the last person Eiddig, Morfudd's jealous husband, would suspect of facilitating an adulterous tryst. The notion that God would go easy on lovers did not die out with the Middle Ages: it survives in modern poetry, and is succinctly enunciated in Charlotte Brontë's 'He Saw My Heart's Woe': "He gave our hearts to love: He will not Love despise." Dafydd pulls off a second, equally clever trick, by deliberately confusing the abusive Eiddig with Dwynwen's would-be violent seducer. Dwynwen was the daughter of Brychan Brycheiniog, who was purportedly the father of ten sons and twenty-four daughters, nearly all of whom achieved sainthood – surely a further indication that the deity did not always frown on amorous dalliance. Indeg is a stock name for a beautiful woman. Cwm-y-Glo is Morfudd's home, identified elsewhere in Dafydd's corpus as Nant-y-Glo in Uwch Aeron.

# *A Shriek of Blodeuwedd*
Chwedl Blodeuwedd

White owl, Welsh ghost,
Pale wraith, a whole host
Hears your sharp shriek,
Thin fledgeling: hooked beak,
Barely feathered gosling breast,
Frail as a foundling beast,
Cleft-faced, elf-shot,
Yawning a blood-clot.

"Sanctuary - tall tree!
Shrink away, leave me
Bearing the curse of Dôn,
Wrath of birds and Gwydion:
Short day, long night,
Crisp cold, grim plight.
Hide in hole, fleeing light,
Bird-mobbed, taking flight."

"What name, which word
Plagues you, grim bird?"

"Fine girl, great fame
Blodeuwedd my name,
Borne of proud Meirchion,
Love-child of great Môn."

"Princess? Words strange!
What man wrought the change?"

"Gwydion at Conwy's tower
Lifted wand, made me cower,
Tore me from my delight:
Exiled to black night,
Once noble, now spurned,
Lust-bitten, love-burned.
By Gronw Pebyr, fair, foul.
Pale girl: frightened owl.

**Notes:** Attributed by all of the mediaeval manuscripts to Dafydd ap Gwilym, but rejected from the canon by Parry on the somewhat flimsy grounds that Dafydd had already written a very different poem to an owl (also included in this collection). The story of Blodeuwedd, the maiden composed of flowers, and magically brought to life by Math, son of Mathonwy, and Gwydion, son of Dôn, is recorded in the fourth branch of the Mabinogion. Created as the ideal wife for Gwydion's son, Lleu Llau Gyffes, Blodeuwedd fell in love with Gronw Pebyr, and conspired with him to murder her husband. This was achieved in a most improbable manner: by thrusting a spear through a standing-stone and into Lleu's side as he drifted down the river on a boat.

Gwydion transformed Blodeuwedd into an owl as an eternal punishment for her adultery and treachery. On being struck by the spear, Lleu transformed into an eagle, and was later healed and turned back into a man by his father. The age-long appeal of the story is partly attributable to its magical wisdom, and partly to the fact that it can be alternately interpreted as a tale of trust and betrayal, or as a parable about free will. In addition to this reinterpretation by Dafydd, it has inspired a poem by Robert Graves, and Alan Garner's haunting modern re-enactment of the legend, The Owl Service. There can be little doubt that the tale is of great antiquity, and the reference to Conwy in this poem, which does not occur in the Mabinogion, suggests that Dafydd may have been using another source, now lost to us.

## *The Crow*
Y Frân

Jousting jester, cloud-high crow,
Crafty billed, and hook-horn cruel,
Dauntless, sleepless, undeterred,
Bold braggart, my old black bird,
Live long upon the growing oak!
Among green leaves a smudge of black,
Haughty of voice, humble of heart,
Watching day wane from a height,
Eidigg of the angry oath
Shall not find you on the earth.

Ebony bundle, free from travails,
Fly, by fortune, a bold traverse,
Weaving through a wood of birch,
Uttering auguries from a bleak branch,
Worrying me with bitter wrong.
From blackened bill your words are wrung,
Your growking grim above the gale:
I must be gone from my golden girl.

Mair protect you, impervious bird,
Dapper of plumage, brave as a bard:
From hoar frost and harm: Mair deliver thee,
From bird-lime and blame: Mair deliver thee,
From the stealth-strung snare: Mair deliver thee,
From the tangling twine: Mair deliver thee,
From felons and fools: Mair deliver thee,
From the brutal barb: Mair deliver thee,
From the pall of poison: Mair deliver thee,
From all and anything: Mair deliver thee.

You would not pilfer, though long left unpaid,
Offal and entrails, for you are proud,
A regal crow, a ravenous ruler,
King of the cornfield, rapacious raider.
Your yawning gullet will not wait:
You cram your crop with growing wheat.

**Notes:** Dafydd's authorship is disputed, but the parody of the litany and the close natural observation certainly match his character.

# Love hindered

# The Owl
Y Dylluan

Fie! The handsome owl's
Incessant speech, sick of soul
Stifles thought, prevents prayer
For every hour stars appear.
All last night I heard her weep
A sore lament to banish sleep.
A roost of bats her shelter
From rain and snow. I shudder
Each night, to hear her charm –
A chink of pennies – meaning harm.
Chieftains my eyelids: to obey
And close them, defeats me until day.
I lie awake, with fluttering heart
And wait for her to screech or hoot ,
Laugh or cry. My heart is wrung.
A pittance from false poet's tongue.

Wretched zeal till break of day
Bids her groan till dawn grows grey.
I writhe tormented, wretched song –
'Hw-ddy-hw' – the whole night long.
She winds her horn to harry, haunt
And taunt the hounds of the Wild Hunt .
Dirty, shitten, with raucous throat,
Sharp as shards her baleful shout,
Berry-bellied, broad of brow,
Mouse devourer, ogling, brown,
Scheming, slatternly, dun and dull,
A shrivelled shriek from a domed skull
Throughout ten forests spilling fright,
Roebuck's fetter, voice of night.
To ape a man's, her flattened face,
Fiend of fowls, her form a farce .
No unclean bird would venture nigh
If once it heard her harping cry.

Philomel speaks less by day
Than she, who gossips night away.
When daylight comes, warmth to follow,
She sticks her head into a hollow.
The bird of Gwyn ap Nudd, her shriek
Bids hounds of Annwn not to shirk.
Lunatic owl! To robbers sing!
A curse upon your tongue and wing!

This song and spell I make, to scare
The owl who lurks within her lair.
Though frost is falling, I conspire
To fill each ivied hole with fire.

**Notes:** Dafydd seems to combine the Tawny and Barn Owls in one bird. In reality, the Tawny Owl hoots, and two conversing owls produce the responsive sequence transliterated by Dafydd as "Hw-ddy-hw" and by modern tradition as "To-wit-to-woo". The Barn Owl, by contrast, screeches. The line "And taunt the hounds of the wild hunt" is literally, "by Anna's grandson,/ She incites the hounds of night" (Bromwich). Dafydd is referring to the otherworldly hounds of Gwyn ap Nudd, mentioned in 'Culhwch and Olwen'. These are comparable to the red-eared hounds of Annwn, the underworld of the *Mabinogion*, who watch for souls about to die, and lead the hunt for Arawn, King of Annwn. I have identified these with the hounds of the Wild Hunt, or furious horde, a ghostly phenomenon of folkloric significance throughout Europe, undoubtedly of ancient origin. Owls were almost universally maligned in British mediaeval culture, and their comparative inability to see by day was compared in the Bestiaries with the supposed spiritual blindness of the Jews. Dafydd, unusually, draws attention to the owl's forward-facing eyes, which not only give it bifocal vision, but lend it a humanoid aspect. It is possible that Dafydd also had Blodeuwedd in mind, since he seems conversant with all the tales of the *Mabinogion*. Magically conjured out of flowers by Math and Gwydion, so that she can become the wife of Lleu Llau Gyffes, Blodeuwedd rebels and conspires to have him murdered, and is transformed into an owl for her pains. Philomel is the nightingale. Its distribution no longer spreads this far west, but as Dafydd is normally such an accurate observer, it is likely that it did so in the fourteenth century.

## *The Fox*
Y Llwynog

Loitering with intent, avid
For love (well learned of Ovid),
I crept beneath the branches –
Our trysting trees: those birches –
Waiting for Her Petulance.
Looking out, I spied, perchance,
A simian shape sidling by
For fear of hounds slinking nigh:
A fox, squatting near his earth
Like a hound sits by my hearth.

I aimed – for it lay just so
In my hands – my yew-tree bow,
Hoping (for my eye is sharp)
To prove well my marksmanship:
As he shot, by ridge, furrow,
To transfix him with an arrow,
This ruddy fox. In my zest
To loose bowstring at this pest
I tugged too hard, more fool me:
The bow splintered into three.

I was undeterred but wroth
To watch him melt like a wraith
Into undergrowth. He loves
Chicken flesh, and spurns the lives
Of foolish fowl. He coughs dark
With his rasping, backwards bark,
Scorning horns, red as gravel,
Loping laughingly to grovel
In the greenwood: there he goes
Across the field, craving goose-
Flesh! Scarecrow upon the hill!
Furrow leaper, red as hell!
Raven-mammal; magpie-hound!
Red Welsh dragon, underhand
Rabble-rouser! Hen-gobbler!
Pelt with teeth! Gristle-grubber!
Gimlet gouging through the earth!

Lantern in the dark and dearth!
Light of footfall, coat of bronze,
Bloody-muzzled firebrand!

No easy task: to follow
To Annwn such a fellow!
Elusive fiend, fleet of foot,
Who fools his foes, leaves them faint,
Like a lion runs through gorse
With a dart stuck in his arse.

**Notes:** One of Dafydd's freshest and most ironic poems. It begins by conforming to the convention of the woodland tryst, complete with the obligatory reference to Ovid's *Amores*, but abandons this notion after the fifth line (I have called Dafydd's lover Her Petulance; he merely concedes that she has made him weep). Then Dafydd flirts for a while with the noble idea of the hunt, before descending mercifully into fabliau and self-mockery. The fox is more clever and duplicitous than he is, and in its wily behaviour, he gladly comes to recognise the admirable qualities of the Welsh in their cultural (and soon to be military) conflict with the English. Had Dafydd lived as late as Iolo Goch, eager Welsh nationalists might well have seen in the fox a veiled description of Owain Glyndwr, and they would only be encouraged by their pursuit of this conceit by Dafydd's willingness to compare the fox with the red dragon of the Celts, who in Welsh mythology is released from a cavern beneath the earth to do battle with the white Saxon dragon. This same cavern is, of course, Annwn, the Celtic underworld, which fits nicely with the fact that the fox makes his home underground, turning him into a sort of vulpine version of Arawn, the poet's weird. Line 33 is very obscure, but clearly makes reference to the magpie and the raven: perhaps Dafydd has observed that the fox occupies a similar ecological niche to that occupied in avian circles by the corvids. For metrical reasons, the leopard in the second last line has been transformed into a lion for this paraphrase. The fact that Dafydd thought the fox was ape-like in form and movement is doubtless not a flaw in his powers of observation as concerns the fox, but it does suggest that he was not very familiar with apes. One can only speculate whether he was also familiar with early forms of the Reynard stories, elements of which were starting to appear in church decorations and manuscript illuminations at about this time.

## *The Frown*
Y Gwg

What is this backhanded gift:
A brow knit, provoking guilt?
A girl gives her frown to me:
My heart frigid as a tomb.

Christ! Can someone make her smile?
Does she frown to make me small?
I hope the cause is not hate –
Perhaps it is some paltry hurt
I have caused her – or she sulks.
Birch trees will restore her sense,
Or if she hates me, the birds
Will sing, make their plaintive bids
On my behalf. Let the lark
Kill her frown, improve her look.
Leafless twigs are valueless
As cuckoos bereft of voice.

I'm in the doldrums because
Of her obstreperous brows:
Their curl seems designed to foil
The smile ready to unfurl
Like a fern. No man's guile
Will spur her to reconcile,
Though I gladly would bestow
Gold coins like flakes of snow
Upon her. I ache, I pine,
I eschew my meat and wine.

She's got six months. Her sweet mouth
Will meet with mine, if she'll smooth
Her forehead. If not, my love
Shall not find me still alive.

## *The Untameables*
Anwadalrwydd

Try fostering a foundling hare –
Not in the wold or wood – here,
Captive in your home: speckle-
Capped caperer, crag-spangled,
Cunning leaper with long lugs,
Crazed jinker, jape on legs.
Still she flees, spurning nurture,
Over hills, wild by nature.

Foster then a sleek squirrel;
From a branch he will quarrel,
Brash, deceitful, fierce as fire,
Far from arrows borne of fear.

Weak as you were, russet deer,
Hobbling by my opened door,
You came for succour; men spoke
Of your tameness, and like smoke
You vanished, bucked your hooves,
Fleeting through the hazel groves,
Rushing deeper through the wild:
Roe deer on the wings of wind.
Run – as far as Iâl, your course –
Race through bracken, white of arse.

Woodsman, tame them if you dare:
Inconstant hare, squirrel, deer.
All shall flee, lest you wound them;
All spurn the hand that weaned them,

And so did she – bright as foam –
Flickered like a guttering flame
And fled: glib bed-forsaker,
Man-dazzler, brilliant faker,
Gaily left love in prison
Sucking on her pap of poison.
Draped in linen, wrapped in fur,
Meek as Mair, faster than fear,
Eighteen she was, heartless hind.
I enticed her to my hand

And fed her song. Fickle, frail,
One day she flinched, turned her tail.

Enticed once to tryst, they're tame –
They'll turn timid, given time.

# *The Magpie's Counsel*
Cyngor y Biogen

Deep in a wood, with longing sick
Making a charm for a girl's sake –
A song of power, a loving round –
As April came without a cloud
(The black-cap among the branches,
The blackbird bowered by birches –
Forest husband, woodland poet –
And the thrush who piped his plaint
Tree-top high, before the rain,
Gold-threaded voice embroidering green,
And the skylark, wise, serene,
Grey-crested, slowly ascending,
Abandoned in the joy of singing
In gyres towards the zenith winging,
Prince of hovering, above the choir
Climbing with a backward spire),
I, a poet, a nubile woman's slave
Sat in the greenwood, joyful salve,
Yet from her memory, weary of heart.
The joy of the trees, a balm to hurt,
Whose green force left them newly clad,
The vine and wheat who defied the cold
To grow, as sun defies the rain,
Left me feeling young and green
And flowering, like the thorn.
There was also among the throng
A magpie, of all birds most sly,
Building – amid the thicket high,
At its tangled top, a spire of spines –
With fallen leaves and clay and lime,
A mansion made for eggs, and sitting,
Her mate assiduous, assisting.

The magpie grumbled from her throne,
Sword-beaked, haughty on the thorn:
"Shut your gob, old, old man!
Belay this vain and tuneless chant!
It is bad for you, by Mair,
Grizzled old man, to leave your fire
And sit here, in the musty rain,
Chanting that inane refrain!"

"Shut your beak! Leave me in peace
One hour, and she comes to this place.
I am in tumult, racked by lust –

The lovely girl will come, I trust!"

"Slave to flesh, 'tis vanity
To rant and rave – insanity!
Despicable you are, and grey;
Don't speak of love – just go away!"

"You! Magpie! Black of bill!
Savage bird who comes from hell,
How dare you interject, and spoil
My spell? Resume your toil!
Your nest is like a thatch of furze,
A creel of broken twigs and burrs.
You think you're handsome? Plumage pied,
Raven headed, beady eyed,
Dressed in motley, jaunty jester,
Your chamber jumbled, chattering joker.
Raucously, in tongues you prate,
Pied upon your wings and pate.
So, blackhead, if you are so wise,
Help me! Don't upbraid – advise,
Give comfort. Have a care,
And for my ills prescribe a cure."

"Sound advice I'll give today –
See you follow it by May:
Pathetic poet, you've no right
To any beauty or delight.
Stick to poesy at your age,
And get thee to a hermitage!"

By my faith, I confess,
If ever I see a magpie's nest
From henceforth, not one stick
Shall stay, nor egg, nor chick!

**Notes:** The poem follows, or perhaps establishes, a convention in which the poet swears to seek a revenge on some animal. The fact that the revenge is out of all proportion to the crime – which is merely honesty – makes it clear that Dafydd's sense of self-irony is at work once again.

# *The Clock*
Y Cloc

Well-meaning, and right-mindedly
I sing. Fate is kind to me:
My soul takes flight to the fair town
With round tower at crag's crown,
Finds a girl, of former fame:
My unforgotten old flame.
Through my Dream, moonlight fleeting
Beams on her a Dream of greeting.
Nightly now, her fetch shall fly
To tryst with me and linger nigh,

Or when, as in exhausted sleep,
My soul, unfettered, comes to creep
Within her chamber, I'll appear
And speak with her till day is near
Like an angel, though my head
Lies pillowed in a distant bed.
Thus my otherworldly thought
Finds the lover I have sought
For age on age. The spell will break
The very moment I awake.

Damn the clock beside the dyke
That awoke me with one strike
Of the tongue between its teeth!
Curse the ropes and wheels beneath,
The stupid balls that dangle,
The hammer, the iron rectangle
Of its frame! Curse its quacking
And its endless mill-wheels clacking!
Churlish clock with canting clatter,
Clodhopping cobbler's chatter,
Lies and treachery in your guts!
Hound-whelp's maw that chews and gluts
On garbage, clapping jaws of spite!
Owl's mill grinding through the night!
No saddler, crupper caked with crap
Could withstand the endless tap-
Tap-tapping of your ticker!
The very angels bark and bicker!

I had enjoyed – until this –
A dream of Heaven, untold bliss,
Wrapped within this woman's arms
My head between her breasts. Charms

Of Eigr, beyond all cost.
*Dong! Dong! Dong!* And all are lost!

Come, my Dream, and seek once more
The airy highway to her door
And set my golden girl aglow
With slumbering love. My soul! Flow
To meet her! Moth! Take flight
And plunge into her orb of light!

**Notes:** Mechanical clocks of the kind derided in the poem were a newfangled technology in the fourteenth century, and are also mentioned by Chaucer and Jean Froissart. Once again, this poem draws on the *llatai* tradition, but in this case, the love-messenger is not the clock, but the poet's Dream, which confers upon him the ability to fly by night to his beloved Eigr. As with Dafydd's other beautiful dream poem, 'Y Breuddwyd', there are strong affinities with 'The Dream of Maxen' in the *Mabinogion*. It has been suggested that the town with the round tower on a hill is Brecon, which, with its marvellous setting, surrounded by the Black Mountains and the Brecon Hills, would seem to be an ideal place for souls to take flight. The poem implies that his soul can only make contact with that of his beloved when both of them are asleep and dreaming, and at the end of the paraphrase, I have introduced the soul-moth motif, which is a common feature of Celtic folklore. Cathedral cities such as Wells, Salisbury and St Albans did possess clocks of the type described by Dafydd, with chimes to mark the hours for the monastic offices, but it is impossible to know with which clock Dafydd was acquainted, and in the context of this poem, it appears that the clock was far removed from Brecon. For a more detailed examination of the historical background to this poem, see the notes to Rachel Bromwich's prose translation, *Dafydd ap Gwilym: Poems*, Ceredigion, 1982, pp. 123-4.

## *The Goose Shed*
Y Cwt Gwyddau

I came once, upon a night
- Ghastly jaunt with no delight –
After wandering wide astray,
Upon a fine girl, fresh as may.
"Have you sought me long?" said she,
"A keen lover you must be!"
"Of course I am! Expectation's
Driving me to desperation!"

Suddenly a savage chap
Leapt, like stag or lightning clap,
Roared like a lion giving chase,
Wrathful grimace on his face,
With jealous ire. "Touch not my wife!"
By God! I feared for my life!
I have a brain, and so I ran:
Pale youth flies from cuckold-man.

"Have you a spur, spiked and cruel
Fit to fight me in a duel?
Else I'll spear you through the liver
With only cywyddau in your quiver!"

I found a goose-shed, safe haven
- Call me chicken, call me craven –
I said, immune to disgrace,
"There is no better hiding place."
A hollow-nostrilled mother goose
With cape of feathers hanging loose
Came upon me – O! Alack!
Pinions bristling for attack!
Brindle bully, grey-lag goose,
Heron-sister, scorns a truce,
Comes upon me hard, pell-mell,
Her grizzled wings the doors of hell!

Next day my love said with tact,
Pursed of lip, words exact,
That indeed she thought it worse
Than her husband's hateful curse
To see an ancient goose molesting
Me! Horrid wails: my protesting
Rent her heart: it distressed her
More than if the men of Chester
Had defrayed me with their jibes.

And now I mutter diatribes:
Mother goose, to save my face
I long to bring you some disgrace:
Crack your wishbone, pluck you bare.
Brazen goose, you'd best beware!


**Notes:** In contrast to his more literary efforts, Dafydd wrote a number of poems which owed more to the fabileaux tradition of Reynard the Fox than to courtly notions of unrequited love. The opening line is a standard beginning for such poems. Even here, however, Dafydd was an innovator, invariably making himself the figure of fun, with a self-irony which is endearing to this day. Given the frivolity of the original, I have abandoned the pararhymes of some of my more measured paraphrases. The reference to the "men of Chester" is present in the original, and is, alas, quite obscure. It seems that in this case the jilted husband had no fear of the bard's devastating recourse to satire, since he taunts the poet that his cywyddau (consonant rhyming poems with seven-syllable lines) are useless in a fight. It certainly seems that they were of little use in combat with a goose. The final couplet has affinities with the horrid promise at the end of Dafydd's poem about the truthful magpie, but it is safe to assume that the gentle poet never carries out his threats.

# *The Spear*
Y Gwayw

I saw a girl, with hair gold,
Shallow waves that glint, fold
And wash her form head to toe,
Twice as radiant as the glow
Of dawn, in Bangor yesterday:
The choir of the Mystery Play
Of Noah's Ark. The deluge swirled:
Sufficient grace to drown the world
With Fflur's allure. Sick I swooned,
Writhing with a mortal wound:

Pierced by seven-sided spear,
Spur for seven songs of sheer
Agony: a poisoned tip,
And Eiddig has me in his grip.
A sharp barb which no man's art
Can extricate from my heart,
And mortal man never made
A spear so fierce, nor any blade
So clear of colour, primed to smite,
Nor could any poet write
Such piercing keenness into verse.
I cringe, creep, and bear the curse
Of Gwynedd's candle, bright as Mair,
The weeping wound aflame with fire
Has scorched my youth, etched my jowl
With lines. I smile a poisoned scowl,
Skewered through the entrails, nailed
To grim love, by lust impaled.
Esyllt's peer has cleft – and blessed –
The ruptured rooftree of my breast.

My ribs shattered, struck my spire,
Rafters augered with desire.
Treason's gimlet in your grasp:
Screw it deep and watch me gasp.

**Notes:** Although she is not named, it seems likely that this poem is Dafydd's record of his first encounter with the golden-haired Morfudd, one of the two great – and competing – loves of his life. The other was Dyddgu, whose hair was dark, and who was, on Dafydd's own reckoning, a more suitable recipient for his affections, especially given that Morfudd appears to have been already married (in another poem, '*Morfudd a Dyddgu*', Dafydd explicitly chooses to love Dyddgu in preference, but it is clear that he wavered in his resolve). All of this assumes, of course, that the poems are autobiographical. The main piece of evidence to suggest that they are is the clear identification of Dyddgu's father as Gruffudd ap Llywelyn, and a poetic contention between Dafydd and the rival bard Gruffudd Gryg, who may well be the Eiddig, or love-rival, in the present poem. The setting is Bangor Cathedral, founded by St Deinioel, where Morfudd is first noticed by Dafydd whilst she is listening to the choir at a Mystery Play. Mystery Plays, which re-enacted stories from the Bible, were a very popular form of entertainment throughout Wales and England in the Middle Ages. There is evidence to suggest that the plays were often remarkable spectacles, with adventurous stage effects being employed to re-enact scenes of miracles. It is possible that the stage for the production of Noah's Flood was awash with water: a visual experience which may have prompted Dafydd to compare the onset of love to a deluge. Since Christ's passion was often also enacted in Mystery Plays, it is possible that the spearing of his heart was the source of the conceit that dominates the poem, and Dafydd certainly seems to echo the erotic suggestiveness of writings on suffering by Christian mystics. The fifth-last line of the poem is my attempt to render in English Dafydd's punning use of the words '*cledr dwyfron*' (breastbone): '*cledr*' also means 'rafter' or 'beam'. Fflur and Esyllt are both literary allusions: Fflur was the beloved of Caswallawn fab Beli, and Esyllt is a Welsh spelling of Iseult, beloved of Tristan.

## *The Window*
Y Ffenestr

Through tangled coverts I crept,
Crooning songs while others slept.
Among ivy clumps I clambered
Outside my lover's chamber,
Pressing on through stem and leaf,
Ardent, stealthy as a thief,
Pulled apart the thick green cloak
To find a window wrought in oak:

There I sought, pursuing bliss,
At the casement, but one kiss
Cajoling my jewel-like girl,
But she refused, little churl.
Designed for a chink of light,
Tiny window – lover's blight!
No magician ever wrought
Such a window, built to thwart
A suitor – unless you count
The one, up on Caerllion mount,
Through which Melwas climbed, afire
With precipitate desire,
Blithely convinced he ought to
Have Giant Gogfran's daughter!
Though I tarry in the snow
The wrong side of her window,
Unlike Melwas, I'd wait weeks
Earning ague and cold cheeks.

If the seamstress of my pain
Were face-to-face with me again
For nine nights, no kind star
Would see the window left ajar:
Despair descends like a pall
Wedged within the whitewashed wall,
Blasted by winds, north and south,
Wishing we were mouth-to-mouth.
I'll catch my death in the sleet
Long before our lips can meet:
Conspiracy of window-panes
Leaving lovers sore constrained!
Where the fennel grows, I lie;
A row of roses, black sky
My companions for my sin:
My pious girl stays within.

Window, lair of prudery,
May a devil pound away
At your casement and your shutter
With his torrid tool, and shatter
Laths, keyhole, and the joiner
Who made you like a gaoler:
May he blind you, eye of light,
And the hand that made you, blight!
Slay the wicked one, whose will
Impeded us, and hinders still!

**Notes:** A humorous narrative of amorous misadventure having affinities with 'Under the Eaves' and 'The Ice', this poem also concludes with a conventionally exaggerated curse, typical of Dafydd's "obstruction" poems. Like 'Under the Eaves', the poem lightly mocks the serenade tradition by making the speaker (or singer) seem pathetic rather than heroic. The Giant Gogfran was the father of Arthur's queen Gwenhwyfar (Guinevere). Caradoc of Llancarfan tells of the abduction of Gwenhwyfar by Melwas, a legendary king of Somerset, in his *Vita Gildae*, and the story is echoed, with Lancelot as the queen's rescuer, in Chrétien le Troyes's *Le Chevalier de la Charette*. We know from other poems that Dafydd was familiar with Ovid, and the subject matter here is reminiscent of the story of Pyramus and Thisbe, who try to kiss through a hole in the wall in the *Metamorphoses*. The poem contains large amounts of parenthesis, which I have ironed out for the sake of clarity in English. I was also unable to resist borrowing the Welsh "torrid" from line 41, and using it as an English adjective in line 44. In line 42, Dafydd describes the girl as "pious" ("llwyd"). It is intriguing to think that this may be a play on the name Morfudd Llwyd, especially given that other poems mention her piety and chaste behaviour.

## *The Peat-Pit*
Y Pwll Mawn

Woe, poet! Well might you groan!
Your lust and hope are both gone.
Dark moorland – clouds casting such
Dark palls! How I need a torch!
Dark over there – sight dispersed –
Dark even here – loss of sense.
Dark below, and woe is mine;
Dark obscures the waxing moon.

Woe to me – the girl was bright
But did not know the sun burnt
Out at dusk. I was made drunk
By praise. Now I reap the dark.
There is no path – sure, my way
Would be no clearer by day;
No farmhouse, lit by sun, stars,
Lamps, lights or luminescence
Is remotely in reach, let
Alone any kindly light
To let me out of this. Poets
Shouldn't try to traverse peat
At night on a rival's land:
My horse has been over-bold
In trotting westward. It's wild
Out here, and a cold, bleak wind
Is biting. How rash and daft
If both horse and rider drowned!

Oceans don't match the perils
Of peat pits! Their stagnant pools
Belong to Gwyn ap Nudd! Fools
Alone would fish them: grim, false
Mires that pulse, bubble, writhe:
Haunts of many a drowned wraith.
I'd rather guzzle ground glass
Than drink this brew for dank ghosts
Who gutter on its acrid
Stench, its reddish, pig-cold clots
Of gunk. My kersey stockings
Are grimed, black, rank and stinking,
Sluiced with slick, stagnant water
Boiling up in a welter
Of grossness – a grim morass
Humiliates man and horse.

Curse the crass idiot who
Dug it, bubbling like hot glue,
Who left me floundering in slop -
When I'm out, he'll get a slap!

**Notes:** Gwyn ap Nudd is the lord of the Celtic underworld, and Eurys Rowlands has argued that marshlands were regarded as liminal places, where mortal men might accidentally find themselves at the entrance of Annwn. Here, Dafydd appears to use the traditional device of the bard's reckless incursion on his rival's land - in hope of a tryst with his beloved – as a means for exploring the supernatural atmosphere of peat-cuttings in mist and darkness.

## *Love's Tilth*
Hwsmonaeth Cariad

I loved, and bore the labour,
And am, twice over, lover.
I fan love like an ember,
And lamely I remember
How love, like a worm, will filch
Hope, and channer through the flesh.

There is a germination
In my heart – a strong motion
Of growing: a shoot groping
From a sown seed burst open.
My labour, ever honest:
To till love until harvest.

Care and woe dogged winter tilth
When ice crystals crept in stealth
Destroying, and January
Brought no joyful husbandry:
I mulched my love, ploughed furrows
For Morfudd, ignored her frowns.
Sharp were the ploughshares which scored
Through my breast and left it scarred
To the heart, and the coulter
Rent my ribs with a clatter,
Scored a wound, sowed my portion
Of love, harrowed my passion.

I waited three months, patient
Until Spring's warmth grew potent
And love took root. It was stout
Toil to fence it all about,
Protect it from slugs. I strove
Night and day – kept love alive.

Nor was I lazy in May,
But guarded wealth, crops made
Safe with a hedge well-planted,
The green twigs plashed and plaited
Together. While her love thrust
Its stem through my riven breast
I did not flinch, but held fast,
Fixed my eyes upon the feast
Of love to come; no shirking:
I whet my steel for reaping.

Grim loss! Great storms came and felled
Every wheat-stalk in the field.
From the south, a veering wind
Seared through my heart, cleft a wound,
And in my wind-battered face,
The stars of love, my eyes, fierce
With weeping, bore heaviest
The rheum of tearful harvest,
And Morfudd's form, refracted
In their wet flood, was fractured
And swam, occluded by torrents
And eyelids red with torment,
The field awash with flowing
Water, my fond heart failing.
The harvest of my heart is lost:
Not a single sheaf is left.

Wind's fury, autumn's rabble
Leaves ravaged fields of stubble,
And fast rain flows from the high
Cheeks of the eastern sky:
Tears for her of Eigr's hue –
My crop all spoiled, and I rue
The day I planted. Alas,
Love brings only torment, loss:
I sowed, yet I failed to reap.
Ruin came, found me asleep.

I am pledged to blight and dearth,
For now love must starve to death.

**Notes:** This poem provides quite compelling evidence that Dafydd was familiar with the 13th Century French *Roman de la Rose*, which also made comparison between the ill-fortunes of unrequited love and the farmer's struggle to sustain a crop until harvest. Indeed, it is known for certain that this text was available in Wales in Dafydd's time, for a copy of it is listed as one of the belongings of an executed rebel, Llywelyn Bren, in 1317. (See Rachel Bromwich, 'Tradition and Innovation in the Poetry of Dafydd ap Gwilym', in *Aspects of the Poetry of Dafydd ap Gwilym*, Cardiff, 1986, pp. 73-75.) However, it is also likely that the poem contains a strong autobiographical element, and that the "storm" represents Morfudd's marriage to the churlish Bwa Bach, who is later to be characterised by Dafydd as Eiddig, the Jealous One. It was not a bountiful harvest for Morfudd either; there is evidence in others of Dafydd's poems that she was abused by her husband.

# *The Bramble*
Y Fiaren

Out of luck – too much in love –
I courted Tegau, a slave
To her embrace. It was more
Than a crush: much like a mire
Of longing tugging me down.
I decided – awful dream –
To go to her, and make
Wild love. Face it: a mistake.

I regret I took that road –
So winding. I can't get rid
Of the memory: my bright yawn
Half an hour before the dawn.
No one knew; no one awoke.
What a futile thing is hope!

Just to glimpse her slim beauty
Is a poor bard's rich bounty:
A bright pleasure – so I thought.
My credentials at her court
Were weak. I knew my sly feat
Could only work by deceit
And not by trust – so my goal
Was to avoid any soul
Out wandering. Poets will
At least admire my stealth, skill
And duplicity. I left
The path. People only laughed
Afterwards: the bold bard leaps
Among the oaks, tumps and lumps,
Traversing miles in the birch,
Midway between wilds and church,
Skulking under shade of trees –
For lust's perfect cloak is leaves –
He stumbles, and his right foot
Is caught on a projecting root.
He flies into a bramble:
Hedge-intestine, twined trouble,
Blighted snare, taut and tightening
Like a maw round my twitching
Limbs – toothy spectre, shame's twine,
Strop of bleeding, barbed and thin!
He flails about, sharply trussed –
Trades a limp for all that lust.

My fall was fast, ungainly,
As I plummeted grimly
Down a steep bank, entangled
In tight, tenacious brambles:
Nasty plight. A churlish snare
Incising a livid scar
On a poet's tender flesh:
Its thousand teeth seethe and gnash,
Mutilate a poet's legs –
Vainly he writhes and tugs,
Speared still more. Its ugly crop
Of bulbous blackberries flop
About on barbed stems, each withe
Ripe for scourging – whips of wrath
Etchers of beech-boles, savage,
Barbed halters, miser's salvage,
Wires enmeshing fallen logs,
Branches thin as herons' legs,
Nets of hatred, archly cast
To trap a man, justly cursed,
Tripwire snaking down a scree,
Harsh string binding tree to tree.

Come, you fires, and raze to ash
These whips giving me the lash:
Burn until the scourge is gone;
Scorch their teeth out, one by one!

**Notes:** Once again, Dafydd's keen sense of self-irony is at work in this poem, not only in the candid expression of his own indignity, but also in his all-too-familiar impulse to take out his frustrations on an inanimate object: a piece of slapstick which has not diminished in comic potential from the days of the fabiliaux to the moment when Basil Fawlty bashed up his mini with a branch. Tegau is not the girl's real name. It is derived from the Welsh Triads, in which Tegau Eururon (Gold-Breast) has a chastity-testing mantle, and is one of the "three faithful wives of the island of Britain". Graham Thomas published a version of her story in the late eighteenth century: "Arthur's sister was wife to Urien Rheged, and she was killed in sorcery. She sent to Arthur's court three chastity-testing objects – a mantle, a drinking-horn, and some slices of bacon. Only Tegau was successful in the mantle-test, and only her husband in the other two tests". (See Rachel Bromwich, *Trioedd Ynys Prydain: The Triads of the Island of Britain*, Cardiff, 2006, pp. 503-4.) If this story is of mediaeval provenance, then it is likely that Dafydd's "Tegau" was his beloved Morfudd, who was by this stage married to Bwa Bach, the spiteful "Eiddig" of Dafydd's poems.

## *Trouble at a Tavern*
Trafferth mewn Tafarn

A fine township! I rode in
With squire in tow, and the din
Of diners, entertainers
Jongleurs, knights and retainers
Took my fancy. Why, I think
I stopped, tarried for a drink,

Saw a slim nymph of a girl
At the inn where I regaled
Myself. She was primed to stun
Me: her face a glowering sun.
I lifted my horn to toast,
Bought her booze and a lamb roast,
Called her to my bench, and thought
She looked up for any sport
That I proposed. My dinner
Went cold, for love was in her.
She agreed that we would creep,
Meet when all were fast asleep.

When the air was thick with snores
I crawled from bed on all fours
To find her, proud of my stealth.
It puts strain upon my health
To tell what happened next. Fool!
I got entangled in a stool,
Tripped, spread-eagled, dupe of fate
Flailed about, bashed my pate
On a table, shaved the skin
In a thin layer from my shin:
All of that, no great matter
Had not the stool made clatter
Fit to wake the whole of Wales:
Ah! The sorriest of tales!
Louder than the Brecon bell,
A cacophony from hell
Broke out then: and when my head
Connected with the table, dread
Seized me – I'll never flatter
A girl again – a brass platter
Crashed to ground, and sad to tell,
The table overturned as well.
To this day, I cringe, tremble,
And hear the platter, like a cymbal

Strike the stones. It resounds,
Waking men, and girls, and hounds.

Near to where I fell, lay two
Stinky English tinkers, who
(Named Hickyn: Jenkyn and Jack)
Feared that I might steal their packs.
Through lips that reeked of stale beer,
One cried out with toothless leer:

"On guard, men! Try to clobber
With your clubs this sly robber!
The daft Taff! He has a mind
To make this din and rob us blind!"

And the ostler, to my cost,
Shouted, aroused the whole host.
Everybody groped around
To catch me. I made no sound,
But cowered in darkness, cursed
My clumsy limbs, prayed, crossed
Myself, relived my error
Time and again, and terror
Gripped me. I called upon Mair:
The situation was dire
Enough. She answered. I crept
Back to my bed, claimed I slept
Through all. I repent! Will God
Have mercy on such a clod?

**Notes:** There are actually *three* English tinkers in the original text, but given the low lighting and his state of inebriation, it is the sort of detail which Dafydd might have got wrong, and Hickyn might serve just as well as a surname. Dafydd does not intend to suggest that these are their real names; rather they are the sorts of names a Welshman might expect stereotypical Englishmen to have.

## *The Enchantress*
Hudoliaeth Merch

Garlands and gold in gleaming
Chains, praise-poems glowing
With love's lustre: all good gifts
I leave beside your closed gates.
Insomnia and sickness –
Despite your grace and sweetness –
Are all my payment, and churls
Crowd me with questions. Such chills
Of awe I felt: your white hue
Like snow – or parchment. How you
Spat your spite into my face,
Called me wretch and made a farce
Of my love! I gave you silks;
You fell into frosty sulks,
Flashed your white teeth in lovely
Snarls, sneered and left me lonely.
Love's plagues and pangs are sweet
Goads: enough to scourge a saint.

Gorgeous girl, I, like Gwaeddan
Pursue elusive golden
Mirages, in hot pursuit
Of nothing, worn out, hard-pressed,
Like a cloak caught in the wind.
Your wry enchantment has wound
Coils around me. Dignity
Deserts me. Duplicity
And discourtesy do not
Taint your pert allure. I doubt
There is any sorcery,
Witch of Dyfed, or surly
Spell you have not cast. Menw's
Magic, treachery, a man's
Undoing: my strength is spent,
Victim of your dark intent.

I'm not alone: there were three
Knew enchantment prior to me:
Would that I had Menw here
So that I could disappear;
Would that Eiddlig, Irish dwarf
Was nearby when you are wroth;
Or I, by the sea of Môn,
Was with Math, King of Arfon!

At the feast, I offered verse
To you. You snorted, averse
To any assignation,
Spreading mist: Llwyd's confusion.

Wise, snide, discreet, you deserve
A silver harp, you deceive
So tunefully. Each note stings
Me. Enchantress, your tight-strung
Harp twangs out untruths, lilting
Lies, siren songs alighting
On sad, unsuspecting fools.
The melody rises, falls:
Perfect and perilous scales
Echoing inside men's skulls.
Carved of cavilling, music
Conjured by Virgil's magic,
Its column is a bludgeon
Which strikes me dead with longing.
Its pegs are pure deception:
Newfangled, and disruption
Rings out as your fingers pluck,
Thin as filigree: a plague
Of plangent yearnings attends
A harsh tune that never ends.

If art, not wealth, rules the world –
Girl-sorcerer, seagull-white
Traitor to thousands, snow-cold,
Pale candle of Camber's land,
Blanched and fierce as any swan –
Take my troth, or I'll be gone.

**Notes:** It seems likely that this is one of Dafydd's Morfudd poems, but it also affords him an opportunity to enlist the heroes of Welsh mythology in support of his complaint. In the Third Branch of the *Mabinogion*, Lwyd fab Cilcoed is responsible for casting a spell on the seven cantrefi of Dyfed: a mist shrouds the kingdom, turning it into a waste-land in which no animal or plant can survive. By remarking that the girl comes from Dyfed, the land of the tales of enchantment in the *Mabinogion*, Dafydd is implying that it is perfectly natural that she should have magical powers of her own. In the story of Culhwch and Olwen, also recorded in the *Mabinogion*, Menw fab Teirgwaedd, one of King Arthur's men, has powers of enchantment so great that should the knights "come to a pagan land he could cast a spell on them so that no one could see them, but they could see everyone" (Sioned Davies, Ed., *The Mabinogion*, Oxford, 2007, p. 190). Math, son of Mathonwy, figures in the Fourth Branch of the *Mabinogion*. He is himself a powerful wizard, capable of conjuring a living woman out of flowers, but he is not immune to magic himself, and cannot live unless his feet are in the lap of a virgin. It is significant that Dafydd invokes Math, Menw and the more obscure Eiddlig in a triad; he is in fact echoing the style of the Welsh Triads themselves, which mention all three men in separate verses (see Rachel Bromwich, 'Dafydd ap Gwilym and the Bardic Grammar', in *Aspects of the Poetry of Dafydd ap Gwilym*, Cardiff, 1986, pp. 115-116). Virgil, too, was regarded as a magician in Dafydd's time. These mythological elements are counterbalanced by the extended metaphor in which the girl's irresistible beauty and dismissive attitude towards Dafydd are compared with a not-entirely-pleasing melody played upon a harp. Gwaeddan is now unknown, outside this poem. "Camber's land" is, of course, Wales itself.

# Love Triumphant

## *A French Kiss*
Cusan

Hail this day! Withhold no praise –
Health to it! It shall surpass
Yesterdays wrought in sorrow,
Eclipse the past, bless tomorrow.
Yesterday's delights and bliss
Filch nothing from the French kiss
I had today. No slick song
Recompenses like a snog.
By God, glorious and great,
How much luck can one man get?
Quick! Give me today again –
I'm glad yesterday has gone!

Blissful moment – so to slip
Beneath the mantle of her lip.
Fair Luned, my kiss-thirst slake
With your lips, as slick as silk!
By Mair, where her tongue has licked
Is sacred! My mouth be locked
To other girls, grimly knit
In a tight and faithful knot.
I remember and I bless
Such sweet virginal largess
Crowning me, gently mouthing.
Rounded as Caer Caernarvon
Were the lips that pouted peace
And put a poet in his place.
Mouth meets mouth, and wetly both
Soon are mating breath with breath.
I was granted – rich treasure –
Her precious lip, and pleasure
Gripped me. So, without a pause,
Diligently I appraised
Her taste. My tongue shall wander
In proclaiming her wonder:
Exquisite mouth! Lips: hot,
Interlaced in Celtic knot.

Blissful battle, blessed siege –
I am vassal; she is liege –
Honeyed tongues that touch and tryst.
Turel shall not have a taste!
Purse your lip, like or lump it –
I'll not snog any strumpet!
A blow – not of fist, but lips
Catapults me into bliss.

Like praying hands, we shall purse
Pouting lips in pious praise,
And may my bright tongue falter
If it should stoop to flatter
Any girl who blights my sight
After Luned's seagull-white
Apparition. Such sweet woe!
Oh God! Will I ever know
Her lips again? Sweat of sun:
The sultry ardour of her tongue.

**Notes:** This triumphant poem forms a more light-hearted counterpoint to 'The Salmon', in which Dafydd's beloved is also named Luned. In addition to this *cywydd*, Dafydd also experimented with a poem on the same theme in the *englyn* form. The reference to the "French kiss" (literally translated "of French aspect") is very likely simply an assertion of the superiority of this kiss to others the poet has received; however it is quite clear from the context that Dafydd is remembering an open-mouthed kiss, so the more modern meaning of that phrase remains appropriate. As is the case in a number of Dafydd's poems, the poet risks blasphemy by sacralising a profane act: not only in his thanking God for the kiss, but also in reference to the "Pax-kiss", or kiss of peace, which in mediaeval Wales would normally be reserved for a special tablet carried by a priest at the Mass. The practice of sharing the peace continues in many modern church services, the kissing has been replaced by handshaking. The reference to Turel is obscure. Parry thought that it was a reference to Hugh Tyrrel, one of the king's administrators: he may receive the king's favours, but he will never receive Luned's. Another possibility is Jean Tyrel, lord of the French town of Poix. In any case, the meaning is clear: Dafydd will not allow any other man to kiss Luned – and, according to the lines that follow, Dafydd will reserve his own lips purely for her. Despite its whimsy, the poem contains some beautiful and inventive metaphors: Luned's lips are compared with a crown, a mantle, the walls of a fortress – and their lips combine to suggest knotwork.

# *Playing 'Nuts In My Hand'*
Chwarae Cnau i'm Llaw

In love's psalter, Ovid said
A lone lover is lost, stripped
Of tricks. He needs a *llatai* –
Good listener, with lighter
Conscience than a bird: a bard
Like himself, a bosom friend
Who'll offer any balm, salve
Or poultice for love's bruised slave.

There was no pair more brazen
Than we two – girl whose bosom
Heaved with a guileless frenzy –
She smiles, and won't play falsely.

My *llatai* began the game;
I moaned. Oh! The sound was grim!
"By Eigr I'm enchanted!"
I cried. That's why we cheated.

*Llatai:*
*There are nuts in my right hand.*

Poet:
My nuts! They're for me to hold!

*Llatai:*
*Hazel harvest – wind blowing –*
*Are these yours? By God, they're big!*

Poet:
Yes, mine! As strong as a knot!

*Llatai:*
*Then you must count, nut by nut.*
*Look and see - and use no guile –*
*The heart of the lovely girl.*

Poet:
Gossamer-faced Morfudd sent
These nuts. I swear by the saints!

*Llatai:*
*What, she who blights all poets?*

Poet:
She is sacrament; I – priest!
Check your palm: five my portion,
Each for a wound of passion!

By God and Deinioel! I grabbed
The nuts and ran! My girl, garbed
In sun, slender-browed, has sent
Fine jewels – no gift more sweet –
For my poem of crafty shape:
Pale cream of the hazel-crop!
Be true, omen! Yea! Amen!
In the woods I'll be her man!
If you're false, then I'm the mock
Of any piqued, tonsured monk,
But if true – why, she shall wend
Her way, meet me in the wood!

Brown wing-coverts of the trees,
Wood-crop, hanging like a tress
Of kernels, rattling in husks,
Hazel-studs, bell-claps for hawks,
Fingers of the autumn glade,
Thrust through green and gloved in gold,
Love's buttons, badges of hope:
Be the hand that brings me help!
No tooth break you, fine pittance,
Good as Ysgolan's penance.
No stone or other weapon
Shall crack you. I shall open
Each shell, by Christ, until these
Wise fruits of the forest trees
Bring her to me, while they durst,
Before they return to dust.

**Notes:** The game of 'Nuts In My Hand' was a divinatory ritual similar to that played by Victorian girls plucking petals from a daisy: "He loves me, he loves me not, etc." The difference was that the lover must have an accomplice (I have assumed that this is Dafydd's love-messenger, or *llatai* – in this case, a fellow poet), who presumably picks a handful of nuts out of a sack. If the number is odd, "she loves him not" – and if it is even, their love is to be consummated. In this case, Dafydd makes it quite clear that he and his accomplice have engineered the right outcome, so that the divinatory exercise is transformed into a spell of entrapment. Scholars have worried about the fact that the Welsh original does not reveal the number of nuts in the hand of Dafydd's accomplice, but the answer seems obvious: the nuts are of the same number as the wounds of Christ's passion (two for the hands, two for the feet, and one for the side). It is almost certain that the game of Nuts In My Hand involved a prescribed formula of utterances. Dafydd's twentieth century editor, Thomas Parry, reconstructs it:
A: I've nuts in my hand.
B. They are for me.
A. Why?
B. Because they were sent to me.

A. Who sent them?
B. My lover, [x].
A. Does she love you?
B. If she loves me, you have an odd number of nuts in your hand.

Dafydd is not the only mediaeval Welsh poet to have based a poem upon this game – Iolo Goch and Ieuan ap Rhydderch did too – but he is the only poet to subvert the theme so cheekily, by admitting that the result was rigged from the beginning, by alluding without much subtlety to the age-long appropriation of "nuts" as a euphemism for "testicles", and by the wry admission at the end of the poem that the whole transaction must be carried out quickly before nature takes its course. It is difficult to think of a more subtly beguiling subversion of the Gospels and the Book of Genesis. It is also possible that the beginning of this poem offers the only textual proof that Dafydd had actually read some of the works of Ovid – he regularly cites him as an inspiration – since Ovid asserts in *Remedia Amoris* that lovers should avoid isolation and seek the company of friends. St. Deinioel was the patron saint of Bangor, and it is surely no coincidence that Dafydd's first sighting of Morfudd was in Bangor cathedral. The exact details of the life of Ysgolan have been lost since the Middle Ages, but it is certain that he was renowned for enduring penance. Hazelnuts were often regarded as little repositories of wisdom in Celtic folklore: a hazelnut, swallowed when it dropped into a river, was what imbued the salmon with its wisdom, and a dim echo of this tradition can be heard in William Butler Yeats's 'Song of the Wandering Aengus', where the salmon has been replaced by a trout.

# *Clandestine Love*
Y Serch Lledrad

Act in love quickly, courtly:
This I've learned. The stealth: costly.

Muse! Help me to find the strain
Which shows most truly clandestine
Love. Confide in no one! Seal
Your lips! Let no secret steal
From out their corners. In crowds
We were anonymous: crows
In a cloud of rooks. None guessed
Our warm hearts were trussed in gold.

Our confidence was the gate
To sunlit dalliance; great
Gulfs between us now. Slander
Forbids exchange. We squander
Hours, wishing perdition on
Cold Eiddig with paltry tongue
Whose words cast an endless knot
Of lying truths: blighted spots
Of rot on our love – abiding
Long as it was kept in hiding.

I walked, in green of leaf
In worship of verdant love.
How sweet it was, love, to rove
Bewitched in a birchy grove;
More sweet still, hand on bodice
Together in arboured bliss,
Together walking the strand,
Together seeding birch in land,
Together weaving tree-feather,
Together taking love further,
Together, slim girl, in fields
Of innocent joy, through wealds,
Onward wandering through woods.
Together smile with set face
Together lips laugh with grace.
Together in the grove, lover:
Together groan, shun another.
Live together, drinking mead,
Rest together on the mould,
Expressing all through love's will.

No beans now are left to spill.

## *Englynion on a Kiss*
Englynion y Cusan

Sun-coloured kiss, cure for age – sore blight –
Treasure of many urges,
Twin touch of praise and purge,
Lock upon the lips of rage:

When I got, for all my pains, that kiss,
The consummation of pleas
Immemorial, her pulse,
Muzzled by my mouth, had pause.

It was Grace gave it. How deft, ardent
And unplanned it was! I laughed
At the meeting. No keen craft
Could plan it. Two breaths adrift

On a sea of berthing tongues. My *awdl*
Of hammered gold intertwines
With hers. Her wine-fed mouth turns
In time with mine. Our tastes are twins.

**Notes:** Only one copy of this poem exists in manuscript form. It was scrawled in an empty space in the White Book of Rhydderch by a cursive hand of the fourteenth century. Since Dafydd ap Gwilym wrote an elegy for Rhydderch, it is highly likely that he had access to his library. The White Book of Rhydderch is one of the two mediaeval manuscripts containing the texts which comprise the *Mabinogion*, and is the likely source of Dafydd's references to those stories. Dafydd also wrote a more developed *cywydd* on the subject of kissing, and perhaps this was an exploration of the possibilities. It is a delightful – albeit overly romantic – thought that the manuscript might preserve a draft in Dafydd's own hand, written, perhaps, whilst he was reflecting on the delights of a literary heritage which could already be said to rival that of the Hebrew scriptures. If the surmise is true, then Dafydd's poem is a delightful Song of Solomon, interjected between the wisdom and prophets of the Mabinogi; a snog sandwiched between the tales of goddesses and gods.

# *A Garland of Peacock Plumes*
Garlant o Blu Paun

One delightful day, at dawn,
I met a girl in mid-yawn,
My mind convinced that the heart
Should craft a wood-poet's art.

I said, "Sleepy girl, come braid
A spray for me in this glade,
Like a stag's branched crown of horn,
As a garland, tined by morn –
A band of love, my sweet bird!"

And the girl answered her bard:

"Bonny boy of hopeful voice,
Peacock proud, with all your verse,
How cruel, to tear the green birch,
And splinter a growing branch!
To harm a twig would be grief –
No! I would not strip a leaf!
Never make a charm of love
Ripped out from the greening grove!"

And yet she gave, by her power,
A gift I'll cherish each hour
I live – good as gold, or poems –
A garland of peacock plumes,
Clean as linen round the head,
Gleaming blooms bright to behold:
Weft and weave of fine flowers,
Jewel of leaves, or butterflies,
Fine feat, crown of creations,
Spiral pansy constellations
Like moths at lanterns, wind-eyes,
Mirrors, Virgil's merchandise,
Lasting tokens, moon-shaped whorls,
Good to treasure, little worlds
Of wonder – girl's gift of grace,
Garland rounded as her face,
Wound like a poem of praise,
Plaited plumes to give me pause:

A love-gift from a lissom girl
To her poet. Godly guile
Enchants it. It's exquisite:
A golden goddess gives it.

# The Cuckold and the Cuckoo
Eiddig a'r Gog

I love her as men should do,
Echoing the song: "Cuckoo,"
Languish under leaves and blooms
With kindred of the cuckoo.

She has a husband. Like glue
He smears her – hates the cuckoo.
He'd spear the bird, run it through –
Deceit would kill the cuckoo –
Uproot birches, as churls do,
Ruin the choirs of the cuckoo.
The clod claims there is not room
For husband and for cuckoo.
Watch: he reaches up to prune
The twigs that guard the cuckoo;
Every branch breaks at his crude
Axe, to expose the cuckoo.

She's there, among trees and dew
Cavorting with the cuckoo.
In summer, against taboo,
I brave the rain: bold cuckoo:
Make a raid on his drooping
Head. Willow hat and cuckoo
Plumes: he'll wear them both, and rue
His pursuit of jays, cuckoos,
And birds of a cryptic hue.
Hide, girl, beside your cuckoo.

**Notes:** In English, there is a direct linguistic connection between the words "cuckold" and "cuckoo". In Welsh, the words are "cwcwallt" and "gog (cog)", so the connection is not so explicit – but Dafydd seems to have been aware of it. The degree to which he was aware that cuckoos parasitize other birds by laying eggs in their nests is open to conjecture. It is interesting that he chooses to characterise Eiddig as an over-zealous gamekeeper, over-pruning his trees and persecuting the wild birds. The poem also provides evidence that Dafydd was aware of the English tradition which regards a willow hat as a symbol of rejection in love: the source of the famous folk-song 'All Around My Hat'. Thomas Parry excludes this poem from the Dafydd ap Gwilym canon because it does not "match his style", and yet there are other poems with a single end-rhyme which he does accept. All of the mediaeval manuscripts attribute it to Dafydd.

# *Yesterday*
Ddoe

God was cruel ere yesterday –
Ever Dafydd's blessed day.
Yesterday – fair nature's gift –
Gave the day-before short shrift.
How foolish that yesterday
Is brother to lesser days
Before it. Glorious Mair,
Don't let yesterday expire!
One True God, give me, I pray,
Ere death, one more yesterday!
You surpass that previous day:
Bless you, perfect yesterday!

Yesterday, old Dafydd got
His own back on the coarse clot
Who injured him out of wrath.
I'm resilient as a withe
Of apple wood; I bend back,
Flex, thrash out, and do not break.
I have the soul of an old
Cat that shudders with the cold:
No matter how the grey sticks
Of my ribs are beaten, tricks
Always save me: so, I stalk
Slowly. Some cats are too slick
For words, but can't take the strain.
Screw them. I'll put up with pain,
Embrace the aches of passion.
I go far, and gold, poison
Or pleasure don't daunt or gall
Me. Pwyll always badgers Gwawl;
Lovers always trounce the churl
Eventually. Love won't chill
At coldness. Morfudd's amends
Did much to massage a man's
Ego. I shall praise her well –
If I fail, I deserve hell!

Good night, girl of the soft voice.
Good day too: you had a choice,
And chose well, upon my life –
Aha! I *had* Bwa Bach's wife!

**Notes:** This is perhaps Dafydd's most demanding, triumphant and audacious poem. He claims to have slept with Morfudd, the woman with whom he fell in love in Bangor Cathedral during a mystery play (see his poem, 'The Spear'). Morfudd subsequently married a churlish wife-beater (by Dafydd's account), who is consistently called either Eiddig or Bwa Bach by the poet. The latter name appears in a legal document of the later fourteenth century, which may suggest that the affair was not simply a fictional device. There are two particular points of interest in this poem. The first makes it virtually untranslatable in any literal sense: the rhymes in the opening lines hinge on the fact that the Welsh language has a specific word for "the day before yesterday" (*echdoe*), and Dafydd rhymes this with "yesterday" (*ddoe*) three times in the first twelve lines. The second is the sustained, punning reference to the first branch of the *Mabinogion*. In that tale, Pwyll, utterly entranced by the gorgeous horse-riding Rhiannon – who may be a manifestation of the Celtic goddess Epona – is almost beaten to the altar by the trickster Gwawl, but ends up defeating the interloper by engulfing him in a bottomless bag and pummelling him half to death in a game of "Badger in the Bag". Dafydd deliberately references this story, and puns on Gwawl's name at line 25, where he describes his feat (of seducing Morfudd) as "dazzling" (*wawl*). I have reserved the reference until later in the poem. Still more audacious is Dafydd's invocation of God and the Virgin Mary (rendered untranslated, as "Mair", the Welsh spelling of her name, in all of these paraphrases), on the assumption that both will approve of the liaison – and, as if that is not enough, his affirmation that he deserves the torments of hell if he does not give sufficient praise to his adulterous lover. Even here, however, the self-irony is inescapable: Dafydd is "old" before he achieves the goal which has been the subject of a multitude of poems.

# Love fading

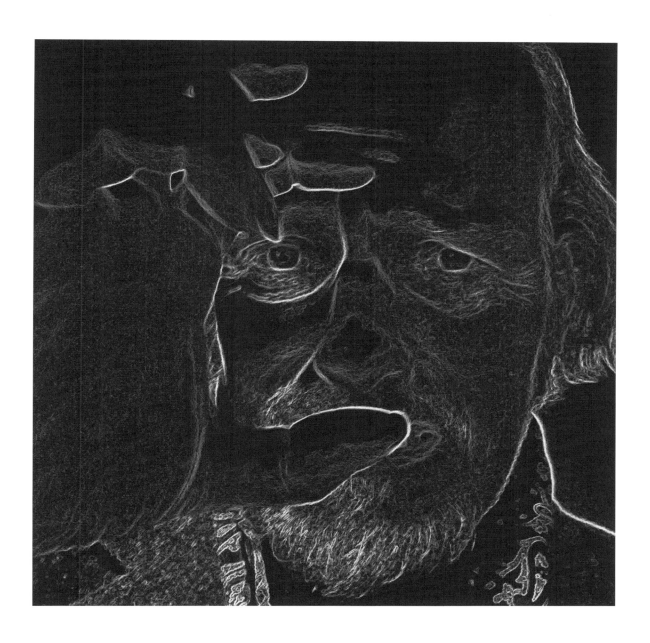

# *The Poet Goes Floppy*
Methiant y Bardd

*He:*
Lovely one with slinky waist,
Royal and slender, do your worst:
Precious ladyship, I cast
My love upon you, by Christ!
Once, you granted permission;
What chance of readmission?

*She:*
How will you gain, with wheyish face?
You must pledge to make no fuss.

*He:*
By your legs – yes, I've seen them –
I'd be silent between them.

*She:*
Put your knees between my legs:
Beguile a girl with what she likes.

*He:*
What, haughty girl, will I do?
My wily tool won't rise for you.

*She:*
What happened to your words?
Deeds fail you. All men are duds.

*He:*
My lust's a husk - winds winnow -
My words blew out the window.

*She:*
Curse the ladies and the girls
You have known – he who beguiles
His way between my white thighs,
Gets me hot and barely thaws!
Take your tool which mopes and flops,
And lie down with fleas and lice!

*He:*
Sleep alone with your wild arse
For company, with Christ's curse!

**Notes:** A travelling poet and musician would have needed some bawdy material in his repertoire, and there seems to be little reason for doubting Dafydd's authorship here. Even though it has been argued that the poem was written by a woman, there are plenty of unquestionably canonical poems which demonstrate Dafydd's own self-irony, and in the mediaeval manuscripts, Dafydd's is the only name associated with it.

## *Sore Trials of Love*
Cystudd Cariad

Love, that old traitor, has wound
Round my heart, wrought her wound

Where once I was hale and high
In the heyday of my hopes:
Painless and imperious,
To all hurts impervious.
My songs were all seduction
And age was no distraction:
Courageous, young and comely,
My minstrelsy was courtly,
Wordy, worldly and renowned –
Cruel of fate to so rebound:

Wilting, worn and afflicted,
In no limb unaffected,
My pride is subject to decay,
My fleshly passions tossed away,
My voice choked. My verses scan
Grimmer than the Fall of Man.
Desire is fled; though she's fair,
Even Eidding has no fear.

No joy wakes and no passion
Rises. Age is love's poison.
No fame or flame awaits me –
*Unless some girl should want me?*

**Notes:** Even when writing moralistically, Dafydd cannot resist a sly wink. I have deliberately echoed Dylan Thomas's 'Fern Hill' in lines 3 and 4.

## *Her Beauty Spoiled*
Llychwino Pryd y Ferch

Once, she was my girl of gold,
Gracious, gleaming gilt – and glad
To love me – but in just wrath,
God has worn her like a wraith
And I am tempted by the world
To drop her. The birch-wood wilds
Call her – yet how am I paid
For love? I should quit, appalled.

It is blasphemous, how spoiled
Is her thin face. Time has spurned
Her. Nothing can replenish
Her colour, doomed to vanish
In dolour. The grief is mine,
Knowing – I suppress a moan –
It is he: the churl I rivalled!
By him, her cheeks are shrivelled.
Enid, it is Eiddig's breath
That blasts you. His lips of death
Smite your face with tiresome speech
And Eigr's beauty is besmirched
With foulness, like moorland murk,
Or peat-smoke that makes its mark
Indelibly. Grim fetter:
Imprisoned by that fat ogre.

An icon, fit gift for lords,
Was hung in a house of louts,
Carved in alder, and varnished:
In lantern smoke, all vanished.
An English fur, fine sable,
Thick peat-smoke turned to stubble.
Fog will absorb, and stun
The luminescence of the Sun.
Green oaks, planted on a groyne,
Wither. Sea salt clogs their grain.

In youth, my visitations
To her sundry habitations
Were my joy. Alas, beauty

Is tenant only: its bounty
Is withdrawn when fools
Deface it. A false Midas fouls
All he touches: Eiddig grim,
Black dog greasing her with grime.

He sneers. My poor lamented
Love, by his lips polluted,
Needs God's and Cadfan's grace:
Succour, heal her soft-hued face!

**Notes:** Whilst we cannot be certain that this poem refers to Dafydd's long-time lover Morfudd, we can be reasonably sure that she is the subject, given that other poems which name her make it very clear that her husband was violent and abusive towards her. Enid (wife of Geraint fab Erbin in te *Mabinogion*) and Eigr (mother of King Arthur) are both standards of feminine beauty often cited by Dafydd. Cadfan was a saint, known for founding churches in Tywyn (Meirionydd) and Llangadfan (Powys). The quadruple metaphors for spoiled beauty in the third stanza are perhaps the poem's most distinctive feature.

## *The Cuckoo Pays a Debt*
Cywyddau, twf Cywiwddoeth

They're windfalls of a poet's
Mind, these bright *cywyddau* of praise,
Bellowing out love's burden
Louder than any organ.
My ribs are a prison cell
Clanged shut on love, for it stole
My heart. There'll be no silence.
Love will serve a life-sentence.

I heaped praise on perfection,
Pursuing my profession
Assiduously. A clock
Tolls less loudly. You can't pluck
A harp to make such clamour.
I've sown enough praise to colour
All of Gwynedd green with growth:
Now love is grubbed out of earth.
"Dafydd loves!" cries every leaf
So all hear it. On my life
I swear: everyone knows it.
At each corner, men call out:
"Who is it?" like a prayer,
Love's questing paternoster.
The deepest string of the harp
Is plucked, like a twang of hope.
Every feast is a surfeit.
My tongue spreads praise sufficient
To make her the prayer's Amen:
Omega, the end of man.
There she rides! I'm love's debtor.
She is Gwgon's young daughter.

Look! I see her, and my throat
Constricts on the cuckoo's note,
Stuck on the same old refrain.
I'll wear a cloak of grey. Pain
Will keep me stuttering, bleak
As a pendulum. My beak
Will have nothing else to do
But clap out: "Cuckoo! Cuckoo!"
A servant to the monks of Môn
Calling out this homophone:
"Love you! Love you!" Fair words, these,
Lucky as a second sneeze.

Plaints tirelessly repeated –
Loving words unrepented –
It's impossible to hide
What every ear must have heard:
I'm employed to use one skill –
To bend my voice, harp and will
To do her honour. She's got
A store of songs – and not
One of them is feigned: seven
Score and seven *cywyddau* – even
More for my bright Morfudd's praise:
Poured out without any pause.
They're all hers: love's downpayment.
Take them or leave them. I'm spent.

# The elements

## *The Enchanted Mist*
Y Niwl Hudolus

I made a tryst with an enticing girl –
A quick elopement was my goal –
Pretty as daylight, potent as doom.
Such delusion! What a dream!
I went out early for the tryst
And like the twilight loomed the mist
The silent spectre strangled light
And cloaked the heavens with the night.

I took one step, and all too soon
Land and sky could not be seen:
No home nor hill, no sea nor shore
Nor birch tree grove in all the shire.
Sulphurous fog, engulfing all.
My curse! You will not lift your pall.
Your sooty cassock cloaks the land,
A choking blanket without end.
The clouds have sunk and spread a mantle;
A black web binds the world in mortal
Anguish: a hellish mire
Like black smoke upon a moor
Straight from Annwn: from fairy fire!
A hooded habit hiding fear,
A gleaming lattice laden with hate,
A coal-cloud smoking without heat.
The day is daubed with dripping night
And all my hopes have come to naught!

Hoar-frost's grandsire, father-thief,
You vault the hill, and further off
From January's trodden snow
You hurl forth ice, and madly slough
Great shreds of hoar-frost . Hell
Has come to hilltop and to heath
Right to the tip of every peak.
You spread a sea, your aspect bleak.
A black magician, there you ride
Hard at the head of a Faerie Rade
Like a crow with a gaping beak
Bereft of colour. Black. Black.
And down in every hollow skulks
A horde of blackened mocking sprites.

There is no hole that is not dank:

A swamp of hell, and swooning dark.
I'll make no tryst, though she is dear,
My lust is quenched. There's only fear.

**Notes:** One eighteenth century manuscript attributes the poem to Siôn ap Hywel ap Llewelyn Fychan, but all others attribute it to Dafydd. The reference to the Faerie Rade is not quite as explicit in the original: the frost is personified "like a world's magician flying/ from the homestead of the Fairy Folk" (Helen Fulton, Dafydd ap Gwilym: Apocrypha, 1996), but the fearful atmosphere is certainly just as palpable.

## *The Star*
Y Seren

Pale as foam, a milky way!
God fans my kindling worry:
Dare I, driven by my love
Seek her in her land, alive
And breathing? Should I elect
A fitting llatai? Elicit
Love by means of some old hag
As messenger? Oh good God!
No! Nor will I bear a torch
Before me, yearning her touch
And gone nocturnal, a bat
That hangs by day. Abate
My pain! I'll go unseen
In light. Night! Come between!

Tonight, without fail nor fault
You'll find the girl, sent by fate,
My gem of bright form: candle
God by darkness kindles.

A blessing on the God who stirs
The cunning craftsmanship of stars
So that nothing shines more fair
Than a pure white orb afar.

Called of God, radiant beacon,
Clear candle, brazed to beckon
Beauty, which can never fade
Or be by deceit betrayed,
No autumn wind, cold, accurst
Can faze her radiant eucharist,
Nor will raging water quench
Her ardour. All robbers blench
To touch her. Saints build her home
Peaking a resplendent dome.
Men do nought but stare, admire
Coveting this pearl of Mair.
Golden coin of the dark
Igniting night-time, single spark,
Armour-gleam, set to stun,
Consort of the day-time Sun.

Proud gem of gold, you reveal
Where Morfudd is, though dark conceal.

Christ may quench you for an hour,
Cast you from your gleaming bower,
White wafer of the sky enshroud.
Fear him not! He's but a cloud!

**Notes:** This is one of Dafydd's most accomplished appropriations of the *llatai* tradition, because it turns the cliché on its head. Dafydd refuses to elect an earthly messenger (llatai) to carry his declarations of love to Morfudd. Instead, he chooses a star for his messenger, and in the process, transforms the poem into a song of praise not for the girl, but for the star itself. Like many of Dafydd's poems, this one wavers deliciously close to heresy in its employment of the imagery of the Christian eucharist as a metaphor for the star's radiance, and in its suggestion that even Christ cannot cause the star to be obscured for very long. The image of the lovelorn poet as a nocturnal bat is not in the original, but is, I believe, in keeping with its spirit.

## *The Wind*
Y Gwynt

Wind who plies a sky-high trade
And scales peaks where none may tread,
Strange your shouting, sheer of fate:
Featherless flight, fleet of foot
Yet limbless, out of sky's vault,
Launched to veer and never halt
About the slope, above the scree,
To sweep and fly, to swiftly flee.
No mount you need, no charger,
Bridge or boat to span the river.
Cornerless, you cannot snag
Or drown, founder, fall or flag.
Nest-breaker, none can charge you;
Leaf-churner, fools chase you,
Never held by law or swords,
Flood and rain are weak as words
To you. When oaks are felled
There's no arrest. You'll not be held
Or struck by mortal man,
Or fire-burnt. No cunning plan
Can stop or even spy you.
Wall of wind: none defy you.
Cloud-carver, brooder of rain,
Land-leaper, breath of ruin.

God's blessing or Devil's curse –
Trees in uproar mark your course –
Dry of humour, tight your grip,
Clouds downtrodden: mighty trip!
You stalk, you slink, lie in wait,
Whirl the snow like winnowed wheat.
Sing me your way, you North Wind,
Come and whisper where you wend.
You revel – when the sea churns –
On the shore and up the chines.
Inspired author, old enchanter,
Chasing leaves at a canter.
Jaunty jester on the deck,
Laughing round the tattered wreck.

The world's length you leap and fly;
By this hill come whisking nigh.
To Uwch Aeron swiftly go,
Audible to all, and blow

Without pausing or restraint
In spite of Bwa Bach's complaint.
With jealous, finger-pointing whine
He had me banished – woe be mine –
Alas that Morfudd won my heart
And I'm compelled to dwell apart,
Exiled from my golden girl:
Go to her house, and rave, and whirl.

Beat on the door, demand entry.
Buffet through and wind the sentry.
Bluster on to where she lies
And in her ear exhale my sighs.
As planets in their orbits whirl
Say this to my golden girl:
So long as earth shall bear life
I'll follow her – as mistress, wife
Or unattained – each tomorrow,
By her faith, in troth to sorrow.
Soar and see: is she not fair?
Swoop and furl her gleaming hair.
Rise and slip my maid a sigh.
Return, treasure of the sky.

**Notes:** The beginning of Dafydd's original is indebted to the riddling poem 'To the Wind' from the Book of Taliesin, but he takes the idea much further, linking it to the *llatai* tradition and metaphorically harnessing the wind as a love-messenger. Bwa Bach is husband to Morfudd, and therefore Dafydd's love-rival. Of all Dafydd's poems, this perhaps bears testimony to his genius for blending tradition and innovation. The pun in the first line is a mark of my own indebtedness to Dylan Thomas's 'Fern Hill'.

## *Cywydd for the Stars*
Cywydd y Sêr

By great God, we made our way
Through the groves, girl, maid of May,
Wandering down the wooded vale,
And your haloed hair glowed pale
Upon the hill. At the bright
Spring we drank. The birches white
Stood gaunt in the dark and cold:
The rage of love made me bold.

I took – sorry is the tale –
A wretched walk through the vale
The next night, and bane or bliss
Set me yearning for your kiss
Since you consented. Sore blight
That I sought the road that night!
I blundered on, deaf and blind
As Trystan when he lost his mind
To love, and strayed, brain in fog,
Through heath, moor and blanket bog,
Crossed enclosures, roughly wrought,
Over ramparts of a fort,
Stumbling down where demons dwell
On that windy night of hell.

A darkling dusk dimmed my sight;
The gaunt gorsedd on the height
Grew black. Blundering in the gorse,
I despaired to guess my course,
By bog embattled – grim pall
Of darkness like a dungeon wall!
I crossed myself, called on God,
Stumbled cold on mossy clod.
My fingers froze. I remembered –
Hope dying to an ember –
A strange tale of scaly-skinned
Reptiles borne of air and wind
Imprisoned in a stone chest:
Like them I bawled, beat my breast –
The bog was vile – pleading, faint,
Pledging to the patron saint
Of lovers, in Llanddwyn shrine,
My pilgrimage. "Saviour mine,
Hear a poet, son of Mair!"
He heard: mercy set afire

Twelve constellations winking,
Throng of stars to stop me sinking
In the mire. Celestial fire,
Bright rush-candles of desire,
Winter berries all aglow,
Sparks that from the bonfire flow,
Autumn's kindlings, nature's boon
Flaming forth to meet the moon,
Sown seeds of the moonlit night
Flung forth to eternal flight,
Hazelnuts profusely poured
Across the sky by the Lord
Who separates dark and light,
Eagles of the glowering night,
Each a sun to make me squint,
Pale as pennies, white as flint,
Gems that grace my God, the Source,
Stud the saddle of his horse!

In the dawning days he strewed
Across the skies a multitude
Of rivets gleaming. Like gold
To fuel ardour in the cold,
Undeterred by wind, each spark
A hole driven through the dark.
Gales fail to wash from sight
The stars on the sea of night.
Through ageless aeons, men spy
Diadems that crown the sky,
Strain the eye, observe in flights
Ten-thousand altar-lights,
Like a rosary unstrung,
Beads across the velvet flung,
Illuminating all below:
They flood the moor, make it glow,
Light my pathway like a stream,
Set the roads of Môn agleam!

I've not had a wink of sleep;
To her chamber, soft I creep.
In my arms she sighs and stirs;
I take my ease, thank my stars.
Love enkindles: sparks have flown:
An axe struck against a stone.

**Notes:** Only two of the twenty-two manuscripts of this poem attribute it to Dafydd ap Gwilym, and it is possible that it is the work of Gruffudd Gryg (fl. 1357-70), but more recent scholarship has favoured the former author. It certainly blends a number of features typical of Dafydd's work. The reference to reptiles imprisoned in a stone chest is an allusion to the story of Lludd and Llefelys in the *Mabinogion*. Every May eve,

Lludd's kingdom is troubled by horrendous screechings in the night, so blood-curdling that they cause pregnant women to miscarry, and spread barrenness across the land. Llefelys advises Lludd to attract the dragons with a vat of mead, and then imprison them in a stone chest under the earth where, presumably, they continue to fight and screech unheard. Dafydd appeals to St Dwynwen, patron saint of lovers, whose shrine was in the church at Llanddwyn – a favourite for invocation by Welsh bards. It is typical of Dafydd's poetry that the speaker sees no contradiction in asking God to aid him when his ultimate intention is to carry on an illicit affair. The final line is a reference to the proverb, "Taro'r fwyall yn y maen", striking the axe in the stone: hard work with little reward. A literal reading of the poem makes it seem as though Dafydd thinks his girl is worth a lot of trouble, but not perhaps to the extent of risking his life upon the moors at night. However, as so often with Dafydd's work, this conclusion is implicitly contradicted: an axe struck against a stone produces sparks: an image of the stars that saved his life, but also perhaps an allusion to the pyrotechnics of his tryst with his beloved. I have chosen to emphasise this more cryptic reading in the paraphrase.

## *The Ice*
Y Rhew

Shuddering beside the wall,
Teeth aquake, compelled to crawl,
Rimed with ice amid the gale –
Night to make a grown man quail
With neshness – not unknown
To me this winter walk, blown
And lonely! But how I crave
The woman coloured like wave-
Foam who hides behind this wall
And has the courtesy to call:

"By great God, are you a man?
Endure the cold! Prove you can!"

"I was baptised, by light of day,
A mortal man, but now stray
By night-time, my poise a sham!
Girl, I don't know *what* I am!"

Saying thus, I fear I fell
On a sheet of ice, pell-mell –
Oh! It was a fateful lapse! –
Water closed on my collapse,
And as I began to flail,
Ice enclosed me like plate-mail.
Sure you heard – you had no choice –
My distant, pathetic voice!
I was enmeshed, because of you,
A fly in a web of blue,
Writhing on a leaden floor,
Locked behind a mirrored door,
Slipping in a sluice of muck.
Slithering, I cried, "Oh luck,
Confound you! Alas, my plight
Is worse here than on the height,
Grim indeed the wound that sears
Pierced by these gleaming spears:
Harrow blades! Each one impales
With the wrath of rusty nails:
Icicles so cruel and fierce,
Wind-whittled so to pierce
Human flesh: fell spikes of dread,
Meat-cleaving blades of lead,
Razor sharp to make me swoon,

Slivered by a sickle moon,
And I am skewered on a spit,
Broiled in bubbles, ground in grit,
Half-severed with one slice!
Love, I am at war with ice!"

More fool me, to walk impaled
By that thistle-sharpened gale,
Inviting chilblains! No boot
Is proof against the ice. My foot
A welt of hot, tingling blood,
Water-wizened in the flood!
A gentleman lost in a trice
Beneath an avalanche of ice!
Perhaps they rescued me, but then
I'll never be the same again:
I've turned feeble, short of breath,
Iced and withered half to death.
Scorned by ice, a sharp sliver
Fatal as a raging river.
Lime that clings and chills within;
Glue that grabs and bites the skin.

My love, coloured like the snow
Can just forget it! I know
That there are better climes in life:
I'll seek myself a warmer wife.
Give me sun: it will suffice
To set me free and melt this ice!

**Notes:** Based on the text available at www.dafyddapgwilym.net. This poem is in the *fabliau* tradition: the reader is invited to laugh at the poet's misfortunes as he undergoes an assault on his dignity in his pursuit of love. Many of Dafydd's lighter poems ('The Goose Shed' is another example) are influenced by this tradition.

## *The Moon*
Y Lleuad

God hinders us – being wise –
In a multitude of ways.
Lovers, lorn and benighted,
Limp on unrequited.

Longing for woman's lightness,
Lust-struck, dazzled sightless,
Slave to Ovid's muse, I stray
Where I dare not go by day:
Lunatic scheme! Sore my plight!
Lost by day and foiled by night!
Luck eludes me, though I swoon,
Love her! Thwarted by the moon!

Waiting in the woods, the murk
Would have aided amorous work
Were it not as bright as day.
Why! Cold moonlight will betray
What seemed a foolproof scheme! Grief
Will get me, like a doomed thief:
Waxen moon, maiden's minder,
Winter-whitened man-blinder!
Baleful, glowering, candle-white,
Blooming Blodeuwedd of night!
Planet wan, a watery waste,
Parish of the ever-chaste!
Half a month, by her rhythm –
At home in her dark heaven –
Will make her wan, pale to wane:
One fortnight clear to wax again,
Then half and half she wavers –
The maid withdraws her favours –
Tide-stirring, bright and wide:
The ghost-sun, the starlit Bride.

No thief ever found a worse
Gift. Moonlit night: burglar's curse.
Eiddig slips out of his bed
At the raising of her head:
She assists the churl to scare
This suitor in his twiggy lair.
Fine florin, Eiddig's friend,
Finding star-strewn ways to wend,
Far too wide, her chalk-white face

Flowering for the wind's embrace.
Faithless, to this lover's cost,
Frigid scatterer of frost,
Faceless foe! My love must hide:
Fear will keep her locked inside.
Fickle circle, fair of flight,
Flawless in the moonlit night.

Candle of the world, she'll know –
Canny creature – where I go,
Compassing the wind-wide world,
Casting light as men are hurled
Callously across the sky,
Careering onward as we die.
Caressed by lightning, bright rim,
Circle of the cauldron's brim,
Cold lamp in an azure sphere,
Queen of gleaming atmosphere.

Day of a base-metal sun
Drives me out, and I must run,
Dart for shelter, ere the dawn
Draws me down for Eiddig's scorn.
Darken but a little, moon –
Do but this – I'll make her swoon
With love-words! Saints, angels, hark!
Would to God that it were dark!
Enough it is that light holds sway
Twelve hours every day.
Good God who made the light,
Grant a lover's gift of night!

**Notes:** Of all Dafydd's poems, this is the one which draws most heavily on the lore and language of the pagan Celts, but with characteristic brilliance, he subverts the tradition by transforming a riddling hymn into a diatribe, and transforms it again at the end into a wickedly wayward Christian prayer. The moon, which might in other circumstances be the subject of Dafydd's praise, invites his scorn because it has cast its light on his hiding-place in the greenwood, where he had hoped to have his tryst with Eiddig's wife. The entire poem is, of course, a witty and ironic meditation not only on the rhythmic nature of the phases of the moon, but on the changeability of womanhood, and his skill as a poet is evidenced by the deftness with which he alludes to the relationship between the lunar and menstrual cycles. Indeed, it could be argued that Eiddig himself is more or less superfluous as far as dramatic tension is concerned: there are plenty of hints here that, under the moon's influence, Dafydd's beloved is not in an amorous mood tonight in any case. The reference to Blodeuwedd – the miraculous maiden of the *Mabinogion*, conjured out of flowers and then transformed into an owl as a punishment for an adulterous and murderous affair – is more subtle in the original, where the line in question reads "Blodeuyn o dywyn dydd" ("Is the bloom of the day's radiance"). In an attempt to echo the incantatory tone of the original, I have preserved the heavy alliteration of Dafydd's line-openings, although not always with the same sounds. It is worth noting that the longing for darkness to cover one's misdoings, combined with a similar incantatory tone, is a feature of the speeches Shakespeare attributed to Macbeth and his wife – although their transgressions were of a bloodier nature. This paraphrase was written on the night of the Full Wolf Moon – the brightest full moon of the year – at the end of January, 2010: a happy coincidence which certainly facilitated the work.

## *Lost in the Mist*
Y Niwl

Last Thursday, when carousal
Seemed on the cards for a spell,
I was in luck: for I learned
She wanted an interlude
In the greenwood: good omen.
"Girl, I'll tryst with you!" Amen.

No man under grace of God
Could have guessed how keen and glad
I was when Thursday came –
Joy at dawn – Dafydd, stay calm –
By God! She was well-endowed!
I went to the tryst, bedewed
To the waist – but a mist fell
Until I began to flail
Across the moor: like vellum
Unrolled by rain down the vale
Or the rust that clogs a sieve,
Bird snare on dark soil, salve
Of blackness upon the road,
Grey friar's cowl that chokes the ground
Quilt to smother the whole sky.
I stared wildly, could not scry
A thing for inscrutable
Mist: earth contused by a bruise
Of greyness, gagging on smoke,
Drowned by fleece from a sheep's back,
A twined hedge of almost-rain,
Chain-mail on the chest of ruin,
Wall of deceit, black as slag,
Spread cloak knitted out of shag,
Gwyn ap Nudd has wound the world
With skeins of night, and his wild
Hordes pile fortresses of cloud,
Scotch my torches with the cold:
All conjured to cheat a bard
Get him lost, and leave him blind.

A rope coiled about the world,
Net of cambric borne by wind
From a factory in France,
Sheet of spider's web! Gwyn' fierce
Face heaves out breathfuls of smoke
Till the dripping woods are slick

With it. Wolves howl. Annwfn's witch
Spreads ointment. I'm left, poor wretch,
To stagger, wet, wroth, ashen,
While the wind whirls widdershins.

I'd rather trudge the moors by night
Than in a daytime mist. Bright
Stars gleam like candles, their flames
Dimly lighting the hunched forms
Of moorland. But in the mist,
Moon and stars are drowned in moist
Fathoms, the bard imprisoned,
Drugged by the spreading poison
Of dimness. Neither *llatai* nor poet
Make headway on the black peat –
And she'll be gone, a dark frown
Shadowing her fine, fair brow.

**Notes:** This poem is very similar in theme and imagery to another attributed to Dafydd ap Gwilym, 'The Enchanted Mist' (first line "Oed â'm rhiain addfeindeg"). Dafydd's authorship of the latter has been questioned, and it may be a fifteenth century imitation, but this poem is certainly part of the Dafydd ap Gwilym canon. It seems at least possible that 'The Enchanted Mist' is the work of a protégé, or perhaps even of Dafydd himself at an age when he was still honing his skills (the poems can be hard to date when they only survive in manuscripts scribed much later than the time of composition). Both poems portray a poet disorientated by mist whilst on his journey to a tryst, and significantly, both blame the rising of the mist on Gwyn ap Nudd, the leader of the spectral Furious Horde, Faerie Rade, or Wild Hunt: a supernatural event which was widely dreaded in the Middle Ages. His deeds are recorded in 'Culhwch and Olwen' from the *Mabinogion*, and also in a dialogue poem from the Black Book of Carmarthen.

## *The Deluge*
Y Dilyw

You've probably heard about
My tryst in that abundant
Bed of leaves, with cuckoo songs
And thrushes as assistants,
A fair girl bedded beside
Me. She lay and sighed, and bruised
Leaves of May in clenched fingers.
The whole thing was just flawless.

The auburn girl was caught out
Right at the climax, by Christ:
There came a great, violent gush,
A clap of thunder, a rush
Of pelting rain, a wild flash
Of lightning. Rent with a gash,
The sky shuddered, and the lass
Grew pale, tied on her head-dress
Hurriedly, ran for her life.
So did I. Love came to grief.

Then the flame-beaked thunder wrecked
Our bed of pleasure, and wrought
Destruction, like a crow
On carrion, struck a blow
Against love, blew through the ricks,
Bull-brazen, breaking whole rocks
To smithereens. Buellt burned
With bright lightning, embattled
By fury in a welter
And mounting walls of water.

There was a wild trumpet blast
Of solid rain, fit to burst
Apart the firmament. Stars
Were quenched. Whole dams hung ajar.
Fear made jelly of my knees;
Rain-squalls were thick as oak trees;
My hair askew. Claps fit to stun
Blew like powder from a gun,
And rancorous as a red
Witch beating basins, dread
Tattooed like a rattle-bag,
A carping crake, a vile hag.

Christ is bursting oak barrels
In the sky. There are battles
High among the cloud-turrets.
Rain cleaves rocks in cold torrents.
Shale cascades, castles clattering
To ground. A grim smattering
Of laughter rends like a drum
With its attack, and the thrum
Is like a gigantic sky-
Fart, done by a monster: die
Or run. It shakes a hard fist
At lovers. Who would dare tryst
Under it? We were alone
With that slug of thunder, thrown
Into terror. Bellowing
Surrounded us. We're following
Our instincts. We run away
When the ass-clouds belch and bray.

Thunder is evil, love weak.
The flood came and did its work,
The wet churl. Lust is a storm.
Neither she nor I can swim.

**Notes:** Buellt is in southern Powys, on the English border, and was where Llywelyn ap Gruffudd pursued his last campaign before his death in 1282. Dafydd is technologically on-the-ball with his reference to gunpowder, which must have arrived in Wales within his lifetime or just before it. A rattle-bag is a skin filled with stones, used for scaring birds away from crops. The call of the corncrake is not dissimilar. The shifts in tense are characteristic of a dramatizing tendency in late-mediaeval poetry. Although Dafydd's authorship is contested, the cleverness of the extended metaphor, which seems to compare the deluge to a simultaneous orgasm, is typical of his work.

# The seasons

## *May and January*
Mis Mai a Mis Ionawr

Grow well, greenwood's chanting choir
In summer's May month, man's desire,
Mare-rider's garland, lovers' reward,
Mastered by green, chained by the sward.
Friend of Eros, bird befriender –
Agape knows him – kinsman tender,
Ninescore lovers' trysts by him
Arranged, to birdsong hymn.
Mair , rejoice! He comes this way:
The perfect month! Lush, ardent May,
Verdant soldier, green and hale,
Arrayed for conquest of each vale.

Clothing the roadway, a dappled screen;
Combes are draped in webs of green.
The frost is fought, the foliage sent
To shade the fields beneath its tent.
My faith, my creed: the chiffchaff's song
As by May's pathway, grass grows long.
Fledgelings sing and jackdaws croak
In topmost branches of the oak.
Cuckoos encroach. Above each farm
An all-day songster chants his charm.
Sunlight swelters, white mist-haze
Protects the valleys from his gaze,
And after noon, the sky is glad.
With spiderlings' silk the greenwood clad,
Boughs weighed down by birds in crowds
On fresh-leaved saplings, lustful, loud.
Gold girl Morfudd comes to mind
With nine-times-seven twists to wind.

\*

How different January: when all's awry
And love is bidden soon to die,
Rebuked by darkness. Depressing rain,
And wind that whirls dead leaves in train
Brings weakness, terror turning frail,
A trailing cloak of rain and hail,
And high tides wreck and valleys flood
As darkened humours blacken blood.
While flood-polluted rivers gush
I long by day for all that's lush.
Sombre, chill, under darkling clouds

Which hide the moon beneath their shrouds,
Sad, black month, good May's reverse:
Turn, return: my two-fold curse.

**Notes:** Mair is Dafydd's spelling of Mary, who was intimately associated in mediaeval thought with the month of May. I have retained the Welsh spelling because Dafydd's Mair, who is repeatedly mentioned in his praise of nature even when he wishes to woo another man's wife, seems far removed from the Virgin of modern Catholicism. Dafydd admired many women, most of them married, Morfudd and Dyddgu being his favourites. In the case of Morfudd, his love must have been requited, at least in part, since he alludes on occasion to her infuriated husband. Dyddgu appears to have remained an unattainable ideal.

## *The Leafy Bower*
Y Deildy

Perfect poets! My Lovely bless:
My golden girl of tousled tress.
"Dafydd, come!" I heard her say
Midst birch and hazel, boughs of may,
Blushed with pride in my private place
(Where else more fit to praise her face?)
A citadel where no one goes,
A living room that blooms and grows.

Slender, shy, she wends and weaves
Toward my godmade house of leaves
Widespread above, loam underfoot,
My home lacks nought but dust and soot.
No drudge shall tread its homely sod;
My bower's made by a holy god.
My girl and I have one intent:
A while in woodland, idly spent
Listening to the birds together,
The poets of wood and dawn and weather
On branches weaving Cynghanedd ,
Who from the very leaves draw breath,
Kindred, innocent of pity,
Minstrels of the oak tree city.
Dafydd shall be the harbinger
And May himself the carpenter:
His plumbline is the cuckoo's note,
His set square is the nightingale's throat,
His timbers are the daylight long,
His laths the pangs of lovesick song,
I his hatchet, she his spade;
Love's altar is the forest glade.

\*

But now the year grows weak and wan
And all my good green house is gone.
I will not pay some hovelled hag
To seek my love in grovelling rag:
Love turns to hate, and green grows brown;
My leafy bower has fallen down.

**Notes:** The poem combines the tradition of the greenwood trysting-place with a characteristic lament on the changing seasons.

## May Month
Mis Mai

God grants that green growth on the spray
Well becomes the beginning of May,
That fine shoots sprout and never fail
When Calends come, announcing May .
Live growth binds me. Yesterday
Great god gave May.

A handsome youth – a prodigal – will pay,
A nobleman enriching me in May,
Undebased the coin he gives away:
Gleaming green hazel leaves of May,
Tree-top florins, free from stain,
Fleurs-de-lys mintings , wealth of May.
Safely guarded from all betrayal
I huddle beneath the wings of May,
And yet, because he cannot stay
I grieve mild May.

I tamed a girl who passed my way,
A comely lass beneath the choir of May.
Bard-father, bless what lovers say
Laud the ones who languish, lorn in May.
Growing honour, greening gain,
God is incarnate in May.
From heaven to the world he came:
My life is May.

Green slopes, fresh woods, long day:
Joyous messengers of love in May.
Verdant tops and tendrils trail
The hillsides – no, they never hide in May.
The night is short, travel is no strain,
Buoyant hawks and blackbirds fly in May.
The little birds make endless talk and play,
The nightingale rings joy round jocund May.
His majesty compels me to obey
In awe of May.

Green-winged peacock perching on the wain,
One in a thousand. King of all is May.
Who could build a fortress, fed by rain,
Within a month, but leafy May?
With green battlements of hazel
Augmented by the slender leaves of May.
Winter with your puddles: refrain.

I'll pine for May.

Gone is spring: this brought scant pain,
Its ore refined to gold in gleaming May.
Summer's brilliant birth, bright Beltane
Makes me weep. Wonderful is May!
Green bark, leaves of hazels, shall today
Be all my raiment, marking May ,
For great wise god has ordered and ordained
With Mair to worship May.

**Notes:** The Calends were the 1st of May, the traditional Celtic beginning of summer, elsewhere known as Beltane. The florin was a gold coin, originally minted in Florence. The obverse was marked with the fleur-de-lys, emblem of the city of Florence and the Kings of France. Dressing in leaves was a traditional May Day rite, no doubt of pre-Christian origin. I have abandoned Dafydd's seven-syllable lines here, and focussed instead on trying to capture some of the echoing quality of the original.

## *In Praise of Summer*
Mawl i'r Haf

Summer in paternal pride
Begets the trees' pleasing shade:
Forest-master, wood-watcher,
High tower, hill-thatcher,
Regal ruler, virile member
Blows the world from an ember.
Summer, source of wondering words,
Dwelling of each spreading wort,
Balm for growing, in a welter,
Ointment, bewitchment of the woods.

By god! Blessed is the hand
That gives growth to branches hard!
Earth's four quarters are impelled
To generate, on sweet impulse
Out of the earth, verdant crops,
Birds that burst to flying flocks,
Hay meadows, blown by breeze,
Hives, humming swarms of bees.
Foster-father, loving help
Of earth's loaded garden heap
And webs of leaves, a leafy graft.
A source of never ending grief:
How soon August comes, the brawler
Who tears down my lovely bower.
To know that all this green and gold
Must depart in mist and cold!

Tell me, Summer, to what place
Do you creep to hide your face –
When you leave, sowing woe
To what country do you go?

Summer answers: "Poet, cease,
Lest your praise should turn to curse.
Fate invites me, fate repels;
Spring surrenders, autumn rebels.
I must grow in but three months
Crops enough to fill your mouths,
And when the rooftree and the leaves
Are bundled close, like harvest sheaves,
I must escape the winter wind,
And enter Annwn , leave the world."

Blessings, tuned by every poet

Fall on you, as you depart:
Farewell, king of idylls;
Farewell, lord of the idle;
Farewell, cuckoos fledged;
Farewell, June's fields;
Farewell, sun climbing
And the plump, white-bellied cloud.

Bright captain sun, you shall not reign
So highly; drifting snow will ruin
Your handiwork. But meagre hopes
Will plant a garden on summer's slopes.

**Notes:** Annwn was the Celtic underworld. Dafydd is drawing from a deep wellspring of Celtic lore about the passing of summer. The deaths of Mabon and of Actaeon, and the place-changing of Pwyll and Arawn, can all be read as myths in which the hunter becomes the hunted, and in which summer trades places with winter, and dwells for half the year in the underworld.

# *The Holly Grove*
Y Llwyn Celyn

Grove of holly, verdant in cold,
Castle of berries, coral-coloured,
Comely choir none can uproot,
Watertight bower, tower upright.
Within, my golden girl inspires;
On its leaves, spikes and spurs.

I? A man whose way traverses
Hillsides, woods with weeping tresses,
To find your fortress, edifice fair!
Through fields and woods I wandered far.
Who ever found, in winter's midst
Green May alive and wrapped in mist?
I found today – I'll not forget –
A holly grove where rooks took flight,
A bower of love, battlements of leaves
Arrayed in May's strange livery,
A columned choir where voluntaries weird
Are piped through stems into the world,
Store house of song, over hostile hollows
Snow shrouded. Still and hallowed.

Fine workmanship, drawn more deftly
Than Robert's landscapes, shaded softly;
Than Hywel Fychan more profound
(Whose forms and metres make us proud,
Who chose the Cynghanedd to praise
The woodland angel's perfect poise
And splendid branches by the verge
With hair of lichens. Verse too vague!)
Chamber of birds born of heaven,
Arching temple, gleaming haven.
My cabin leaks and drips all night;
The holly bower is watertight.
Edged with steel, the leaves unwithered
Rarely rusted, never weathered.
From here to Severn , no old goat
Would chew on these, his teeth to grate
A muzzle of spines . Night looms long
And moorland mist hangs in the lung,
But wind and frost will not deprive
The handsome holly of his tithe:
While birches wither, oak trees rot,
Holly becomes my Camelot.

**Notes:** Robert is an unidentifiable painter, and Hywel an unidentifiable poet. Dafydd's poems are set in the rough triangle of land between Aberystwyth, Tal-y-Bont and Ponterwyd. The "muzzle of spines" is an allusion to the spiked leather muzzle which was used to prevent the calves of milk-cows from suckling.

## *Stealing Summer*
Lladrata Haf

A source of joy: being at work
In the woods, the glade awake
With singing. The afternoon
Rang out with the bright refrain
Of a jocund thrush, whose voice
Chimed above my head, the verse
Of the verdant canopy,
News to thrill the heart of me:

"Fine advice I have to give:
Whilst it is May, frolic, live
Each day in a fort of birch
Fine as any house or church,
Beneath your head, a pillow
Feathered with leaves of willow;
Above your head, where I fly,
Traceries of twigs and sky."

I do not ail: that is good.
I am not hale: swear to God.
I am not dead: Peter's plea.
I do not live: God's decree.
I am not blessed, nor am cursed:
To be either, gift of Christ,
Would be fine: to die, or live
Lapped in leaves of splendid love.

Time has been, Christ dare not steal
Summer from me. All turns stale.
Time has been, I was alive.
The sere has come. None can thrive.

## Winter-Courting
Caru yn y Gaeaf

Woe to the fool who courts out
Of season. Summer's account
Is in the red. Dreadful thought:
I sought a girl; winter taught
Me a lesson. Snow is fraught
With danger. Cold Yule has brought
The result: too farcical!
I'm the dupe of icicles.

In fine frame of mind, I came
Drunk, to a tavern (I blame
Only myself) full of zeal,
All set – so it seemed – to steal
Her affections. She was bright,
Alluring. And in the night
I missed that keen, dripping shard
Of ice, unsheathed in the yard.
It dripped right into my face
A great gob of molten frost,
Cold whistle, bright spout of phlegm
Eiddig's candle, guttering rheum,
Nasty branch of a grim oak,
Harrow blade, glistening rake,
Frozen tears which made me stagger
Onto the grim ice-dagger:
The icicle wins: my plan, a wreck –
It stabs deep into my neck.

I made the signal: I tapped
On the window. Zounds! A trap!
Light-sleeping Eiddig awakes
Sooner than she does, and shakes
Her, pokes my girl down below
With his clammy, cold elbow
(Thinking that some youthful rogue
Seeks to steal his cash). And rough
Was his voice, the withered churl,
Shouting vengeance! The stench whirled
About him, stale as old farts.
He leapt from bed with a start
And with grim voice, hoarsely roused
All denizens of the town
To hot pursuit. The boor wails,
"Lo! A thief! And here's his trail!"

And with an altar-candle, leads
A hundred men. I baulk, flee,

And am running, in a trice,
Along a daunting ridge of ice,
Seeking shelter in the bower
That shielded us from the showers
Of summer: the wood in leaf
Was sure to bring me some relief –
The birds who in sun-blest play
Frolicked where we met in May
Would be my guardians! Vain thought –
For in the woody grove was nought
But desolation. Relief
Was nowhere, and not one leaf
To shield a man: the green crown
Usurped by winter – cast down
For mouldering. I implore
For May to come, bring the thaw!

Winter's prisoner, I pray
For leaves, and a summer's day!

**Notes:** This poem brings together a number of signature-features of Dafydd's verse: the self-ironic narrative, the scornfully comical portrait of the cuckold Eiddig, the curse-like characterisation of the icicles through a string of metaphors, and the seemingly random shifts in tense which lend themselves to oral performance. The praise of early summer at the expense of the winter months is another theme which is commonly encountered in Dafydd's verse, but even this serves the beguiling cause of his self-irony, since the privations of winter are the inspiration for some of his best poems.

## *Cywydd to the Snow*
Cywydd yr Eira

How boring to be housebound,
Pained, drowsy, hebetated:
No wood, common, road or hill
Is clear. Snow has sapped my will,

For should some girl's word beguile
Me from my house, I'll bewail
My plight before long. A plague
Of falling feathers will plunge
Upon me. I'll lunge, murmur
Like a grim dragon-mummer,
White as a miller. The year
Turned. Now everyone wears fur.

In January, our habits
Anger God: he makes hermits
Out of us: no holy wish
Can save us from the whitewash.
There's no grove but wears a sheet,
The ground smothered by the sleet.
Every branch is garbed in fur
Or flour: white April flowers
Are less abundant. Will God
Blow the goose-down from the glade?
In Gwynedd there's no haven
Safe from the bees of heaven,
The black ground festooned with foam,
Clods of fleece upon the loam.
We all succumb to a fierce
And dauntless invading force,
The whole earth beneath a crust
Ice-fashioned by angel-craft.

It's as though the silo-plank
Were pulled away. Angels pluck
It sideways, and with a gush,
The flour falls in one great rush.
Its cold cloak muffles ditch, hill,
Plugs with mortar every hole,
The greenwood grove all agleam,
Choking in a cloud of lime,
Gravel, covering field, hollow,
With a skin of pale tallow,
As if the angels' ardour
Had plated all with armour.

And then the snow starts to drift,
Scatters all the tracks with dust,
Leaps like a lad, ermine clad
O'er heather, immune to cold:
His skirts avalanche the lee,
Pave it deeper than the sea.

Walls of snow in every shire –
One great sheet from shore to shore –
A great spilling of the earth's
Brains, in some battle of dearth.
White palsy! All my pleasure
Encased in magic plaster,
Leaving all my plans in ruin!
God – refrain! Bring on the rain!

**Notes:** Thomas Parry excluded this from the Dafydd canon, thinking it was fifteenth century work, but more recent scholars have questioned his judgement on this and a number of other poems. The disdain for winter because of its adverse effects on amorous play is certainly a common enough theme of Dafydd's verse, but may also have been attractive to his imitators. Line 8 is of particular interest, since it contains a rare reference to mediaeval Welsh drama – most likely a mumming play, since some English mumming traditions involve the wearing of feathers to represent the scales of a dragon. Ermine is, of course, the fur of the stoat, which turns white in winter (apart from the black tail-tip), providing a particularly exquisite trimming for the robes of the nobility.

# *Summer*
Yr Haf

Since Adam's sin encumbers
Us, the shortness of summer's
Surge is rough justice. Glamour
Fades: a scourge of summer,
Whose still sky all a-glimmer
Glints with sun's fire of summer.
Its dome could not be clearer
Above the world. Bless summer!

Good crops, flesh clear as amber,
Grow from old mould in summer.
Comely green vines can clamber
Over trees, drawn by summer.
The birch tree's hair grows greener
And makes me laugh for summer:
It crowns me heaven's singer
With chortling songs of summer –
I praise it, strong with pleasure:
Sweet, satisfying summer!

She's keen – of sea-foam's colour –
My tree-nymph girl, in summer.
The cuckoo is my server
At my request, in summer –
His tongue a fine bell-clapper
I bid to toll for summer.
The nightingale sings sweeter
Made brave by leaves of summer.
On long days, Ovid's charmer
Cuckolds with ease in summer:
Snide Eiddig need not bother
With guarding her – till summer:
He is custom-built for winter,
But lovers live for summer.

Birch-bound, and unencumbered
By any want but summer,
I dress in pure gossamer –
The filaments of summer –
Untwine the ivy. Thunder,
Cold: stay away – it's summer!
I tell my girl, "Creep closer,
My naked love, in summer."

All satires are rank failures:
For spite can't thrive in summer –
But what's this wind? I shiver –
For yesterday was summer.
My heart is all a-flutter
That clouds should steal my summer.
In snow and ice, I shudder
When autumn dispels summer:
And Christ shall hear me clamour:
"Where did you hide my summer?"

**Notes:** The transitory nature of summer was a favourite theme not only for Dafydd, but also for a number of poets who imitated him, but the fourteenth century Welsh rings in this poem with a consummate mastery which is a strong argument for authenticity. The Welsh word for summer is "haf", and this syllable ends every second line, allowing the poet to choose from a range of rhymes with unstressed "-af" endings every other line. This effect is impossible to achieve in English, but pararhymes do at least give an impression of the subtlety of the original. The monorhyme is a feature of a number of Dafydd's poem, including his marvellous evocation of the month of May. Eiddig is the name of Dafydd's love rival, the skulking Bwa Bach who married his beloved Morfudd, but on the evidence of poems such as this one, failed to win her undivided affection. Particularly effective devices here include the suggestions of nakedness, and the fleeting adoption of the cuckoo as a *llatai*, or love messenger – since cuckoos are migratory, and only sing for a month or two. Dafydd is clearly alive to the allegorical possibilities presented by a wet summer such as the one we are having this year. A promising summer can be cut short; so can a promising life.

# Self-evaluations

## *The Heart*
Y Galon

Heart, who runs beck-full with blood,
Round of head and over-bold,
Chunk of flesh, plumbed for pity,
Red pump-room of poetry,
Sanguine pilgrim, ribcage-bred,
Meat of life for bird and bard,
Plump pound of passion, pride's pulse,
Gospel parcelled in a purse:
Pound out the truth, egglike shape!
Make peace! Call truce! Barbs as sharp
As love may pierce you. My breast
Flows with verses, fit to burst,
A roaring torrent. Love's plaints
Turn wantons into poets.

Stop. Let us consider mead:
Purest liquor will demand -
Much like love - full-gushing flows
Of largesse. Flush waterfalls
Run with less. And divested
Of his cash, the dull drunkard,
His cock gone floppy, its bold
Head poking from his pants, cold
And clammy, gains nothing much,
But a sore head, and a crutch
To keep him upright. So bold
He was, he cursed a man's beard,
Got clobbered, fornicated
With a maid. His inflated
Lust was punctured and he failed.
Love's like that: the fair is fouled.

Heart! Don't deceive! It's disease,
This love-blight! It spreads, devours
My blood like drunkenness. Beast
I have become! My caged breast
Clangs closed on my pulsing soul.
Disapproval's set to spoil
It all. Everyone admires
Her, orblike as a rising
Moon, my Morfudd. One bat
Of her eyes: you miss a beat
Like a sun eclipsed. Her lips,
Parted, would induce a lapse

Enough to kill. How I hate
My poor, drunken, pumping heart!

## *The Mirror*
Y Drych

I never dreamed – O! Whoreson! –
That I was aught but handsome
But holding glass in hand –
O vile! I take it hard!
It tells the truth, I fear:
My face is far from fair.

Grown pale from Enid's peer
My cheek grows white, like poor
Glass, each facet flawed,
With livid weals defaced.
My nose is a prosthetic,
Razor long – pathetic!
A gimlet gouged the holes
That hold my eyes. My hairs
Fall in handfuls, mocking
This hell of my own making.

Villainous my fate,
I'm staring at defeat.
A wayward arrow flies
Or else the mirror lies.
The flaw is mine indeed –
Then let me be dead! –
No warp within the glaze:
A pox upon this glass!

Enchanted, pale round moon,
An orb for men who mourn,
Magician's pearly perjurer,
A dream of palsied pallor
Reflecting only dolour,
Ice-brother, cold deceiver,
Queasy-coloured masquer –
To hell with you, warped mirror!

If glass can tell the truth,
These wrinkles, by my troth,
Were got from a Gwynedd lass
Who laughs and spoils men's looks.

**Notes:** Perhaps Dafydd's great masterpiece in the genre of self-deprecation.

## *Englynion: Lament for Greying Hair*
Englynion Bardd i'w Wallt

This very day, my mirror showed – how grim
Is the way life fades – a shred
Of sad grey hair. Oh! It stirred
Grief! How sneakily it appeared!

My blond locks have been augmented – how vexing –
Youthful memory won't mend it –
With growths of grey. What made it
Lovely – colour – now mars it.

The glass was flawless, not lying – too harsh
Its taunting. Now, fear's cloying
Finger grips me: white hair filling
Me with memory's coloured longing.

It was copious and gold – my hair –
Fine sight, it made me glad.
Now, my hopeful heart is ground
Between stones. Grey age has gained.

Colour in my locks: a bloom short lived.
It withers quickly. I blame
Nature. There is no bright balm
Can bring back that clear blond gleam.

Once, I wore a yellow veil – like gold –
Fine sight. Consonants and vowels
Are useless. The glass reveals
Aged hair: ugly, grey. Vile!

**Notes:** This sequence of *englynion* is one of several pieces of evidence which suggest that Dafydd survived at least the initial outbreaks of the Black Death and lived into old age, at least by fourteenth century standards (another is a poem in which he laments the effects of age on his beloved Morfudd). It also bears comparison with 'The Mirror' – a poem in which the sense of self-irony is delivered with a lighter touch. All of Dafydd's poetry makes frequent use of *sangiadau*, or parenthetical phrases. In this paraphrase, I have retained these more faithfully than usual, partly because the *englyn* verse form requires it, with its subordinate clause at the end of each first line, and partly also because it seems to suit the subject.

## *Love Like a Fowler*
Yr Adarwr

The fowler, after a frost,
Or flurries of snow, comes first
Along the path, setting traps
Where the moon shines on hilltops.
His honeydew and coltsfoot
He blends, like a cruel craftsman,
And smears glue of mistletoe
On twigs above the melt-flow,
And birds come from distant shores
To Môn. Suffering is sure.

A bird looks down, flying free
Above the grey estuary,
And comes to land, bright with glee,
But finds its plumes glazed in glue.
It writhes: is limed more firmly,
And dies, prey to the fowler.

Likewise God, king of what lives,
Is the cruel fowler of loves.
Hillside snow is a girl's face:
A fine blizzard, white and fierce.
The melt-waters are the tears
Of my Eigr, who betrays
My troth, her eyes like berries,
Jewels of Christ. Her treason brews
A hundred sighs. Close, you eyes –
Snap shut like brooches. No more lies!
She loves me not, but limes me,
Her smile, a glue that slimes me
Into silence, yet my love
Will not leave me, while I live,
But plague my mind, keep it drunk
Till it is consumed by dark.
I sing her colours – bold bard –
And finish like a limed bird.

Love is a trap: lures the mind
To lingering death. It's murder.
Her eyebrows are the twigs, slimed
By plucking into fine, slim
Lines. Lashes flutter: blackbirds'
Wings. Her eyelids close like blinds,
Or clouds, blacking out the love,
And leaving me half alive,

Nailed in place, limb upon limb:
Love's memories cling like lime.

**Notice:** The cruel practice of bird-liming (still, unfortunately, prevalent in some European countries, and a great peril to migrating birds) involves the smearing of twigs with a sticky substance, often derived from the mucilage in plants such as coltsfoot and mistletoe. When birds alight on a branch, they find themselves stuck to it, and in their struggles, ensnare themselves still more as their feathers come in contact with the 'glue'. Shakespeare would later put the metaphor of the 'limed soul' into the mouth of Claudius – a man cut off forever from repentance and salvation because his own wife was once married to the man he murdered – but Dafydd had used the analogy two centuries earlier.

## Needles in the Eye
Nodwyddau Serch

Although you gleam like Indeg,
My love's a grief unending:
Nine years' torment, tiresome load
A shackle on a strong lad.
Love is like a foster son
Who goads his good father on
To despair: a murderer,
A worthless, spoilt marauder.

All I gain from love, Morfudd,
Is a gift of maddening grief.
Every Sunday, and on feasts,
I follow you to church, fists
Clenched in anguish, pale-faced girl,
And there, like a glinting grail
You stand, and I, sentinel
Of sad, lovelorn lust, stand still,
My wide eyes compelled to grope
Your body, fast in its grip.

Sharp needles – a dozen, say –
Span my eyelids every day,
Pried open – tears like a lake –
So I am compelled to look.
Your golden form keeps them pressed
Open, needled wide apart,
And welling up from my fond
Heart, rheum in a flood
Overflows, my humours
Out of balance. Sad horrors
Assail me, and fond desire
Finds me floundering in despair.
Gall swells up and grips my throat:
Girl, you give it not a thought,
And like battle-blood, my tears
Well up fast, and stain my beard.

Though I stay to hear a psalm
On Sunday, it's your bright, slim
Form I worship. Not all girls
Think me gormless. Your cruel guiles
Compel you, by love's own laws:
Girl, relent, and make me yours!

**Notes:** One of Dafydd's frankest admissions of outright lust – and they were not few and far between – this poem also employs one of his most arresting images. Indeg, according to the Welsh Triads, was one of King Arthur's three concubines, and Dafydd refers to her in five separate poems as an ideal of feminine beauty. (Triad 57: See Rachel Bromwich, *Trioedd Ynys Prydain*, Cardiff, 2006, pp. 164 and 404-405.)

## *My Shadow*
Ei Gysgod

Yesterday, while under leaves
Awaiting my Helen, in love's
Thrall, beneath birches, eluding rain,
I stood, a Fool, courting ruin.
At once, I saw a looming form
Most ugly, with stooping frame:
I shied from it, and shrugged,
Invoking saints. Stark and ragged,
It goaded me. I made prolonged
Prayers for deliverance from plague.

*The poet:*
"Speak to me, you silent wraith –
Say who you are, O thing of wrath!"

*His shadow:*
"Question not, you quailing fool!
I am your shadow, gaunt and frail.
By Mair, I bid you, not a sound,
But silence, till you understand!
A naked entity I am, your weird,
And wait upon you with my word:
You think yourself a jewel? My curse
Upon you, animated corpse!"

*The poet:*
"You lie, you goblin, evil sprite
Sent to taunt me for your sport,
Bleating goat with buckled back,
Mocking mimic of man! Black
Phantom! Dissimulating imp!
Grim parody! Simpering ape!
Burly troll on shaking stilts,
Withered thing on witch's shanks,
Boggart-shepherd, besmeared in muck,
Glabrous as a tonsured monk!
Jockey's joke on obby oss,
Heron-legged, obtuse, obese
Crane spanning half a field
Leaving crops and lands defiled!
Prating pilgrim, fatuous of face,
Blackened friar, stalking farce,
Corpse within a hempen shroud,
Why speak a word, deceiving shade?"

*His shadow:*
"I have been – watch what you say –
In step with you for many a day."

*The poet:*
"Liar with your milk-churn neck
With what libel would you knock
Me down? With sin untainted
I mock you for a devil's turd!
I have no treason in my heart,
I never backstab. I haven't hurt
A chicken with a sling or stone,
Or pestered children. Not one stain
Besmirches me. I never moan
When spurned by wives of other men."

*His shadow:*
"If all I've seen were said
I swear you'd not be saved:
In no time you'd be lurching
In a wagon, to your lynching."

*The poet:*
"Stop! Unstring your snare!
Say nothing! Do not sneer!
If I had you in my grip
I'd stitch you lip to lip!"

**Notes:** A parody of a traditional mediaeval genre: the dialogue between Body and Soul. "Helen" is not the name of the beloved, but a reference to Helen of Troy, whose beauty also brought ruin.

## *A Dozen Reasons for Preferring a Poet to a Soldier*

Merch yn Edliw ei Lyfrdra

Slender, tentative lady
In gilt and jewels, with shady
Eyes, Eigr with augrim stones
Will not reckon what she owes.
I reproach her 'neath the leaves:
"Shining jewel who never loves,
I sing your praise, smooth as milk,
Eight times bright as spider-silk."

*She:*
"You are easy to renounce:
Love is dull, worth not an ounce
Of basest metal, Dafydd:
It would only make me laugh if
Your were mine, craven coward."
Thus she scoffed, fickle, froward.

*He:*
"Gossamer-clad, choosy one,
Determined to do me wrong.
I am genial, a charmer –
A coward, true, without armour –
But in the arbour, Ovid scores:
I'm valiant in *amores*!

Eigr's rival, you scarce know me,
But for *cywyddau*, sure you owe me!
Besides, I count at zero
Dauntless love for some hero:
Grim thought – I know, it's tough –
A soldier's love is always rough,
For he loves war (that's scary),
Every way a mercenary.
Should he hear in Scotland, France,
Of battle, he'll advance,
Seek adventure there instead,
Forsake manoeuvres in your bed.
And what then? Should he survive,
Thrash the French, escape alive
From the crossbows as they shoot,
He'll return a scarred old brute.
He prefers his sword and lance
To you – don't look askance –
And his corselet and shield,

And his stallion, roaring "Yield!"
Should you smart, he'll not protect:
He'll tup you and show no respect.

With witty words I'm well endowed
Enough to strip your silken shroud
And weave instead a robe of praise –
Then gaze upon you all our days.
Were I to conquer kingdoms rich,
Deifr's charms would yet bewitch
Me. I'd give them all, and run,
Embrace the splendour of the sun."

**Notes:** As he implies in line 20 ("Llwfr wyf ar waith llyfr Ovid"), Dafydd is indebted here to Ovid's *Amores* iii, 8, in which the poet tells a girl she is stupid for loving a soldier in preference to him, but as always, he makes the theme his own by adopting a measure of self-irony, and by sly references to the phallic nature of a mediaeval soldier's weaponry. He compares his beloved to Eigr (Ygraine in the Arthurian cycle), the mother of Arthur, who had direct experience of a soldier's unwanted advances, but later casts her in the mould of Deifr, one of the maidens in Arthur's court. The references to wars with the French make it probable that Dafydd is deliberately juxtaposing chivalric ideals with the martial realities of his own lifetime. Accordingly, in my paraphrase I have armed the French with the crossbow: a killing machine which proved disastrously less efficient than the English longbow at the Battle of Crécy in 1346. Indeed, Ifor Williams has suggested that line 48 is an ironic reference to the hubris of Edward III after his victory at Crécy and his conquest of Calais. Rachel Bromwich has suggested that the word *awgrym* is "derived from the name of the Arabic inventor of Algebra, used by extension to denote the Arabic system of numerals, and hence 'arithmetic'. 'Augrim stones' were used for counting; hence Dafydd asks the girl to reckon what she owes him, presumably for his poems to her." I like to think that Dafydd is implying that the girl is counting up the pros and cons of the soldier on an abacus, or on her rosary beads. Perhaps a Latinate pun is also intended, since the identification of the girl with the sun at the end of the poem suggests that, like Morfudd, she is a "golden girl". A more far-fetched interpretation – albeit a pleasing one – is that the girl is attempting to read love auguries by casting stones.

## *Love's Journeyman*
Taith i Garu

Who else has toiled in travel,
Worn with tyrant love's travail,
As I have? Hoar-frost, wind,
Snow and rain: through these I wend
My heedless way, at her word.
Fatigue is my one reward:
My feet drag in Cellïau'r Meirch
Drawn by her across Eleirch
And barren moors, day and night;
She is never once in sight.

"Oh my God," I bawl it out
In Celli Fleddyn – grim shout –
Plaintively professing love,
Yet she barely knows I live.
Bysaleg, a babbling brook,
Water churning at the bank ,
I ford each day for her sake –
Cold christening – then I seek
Her – not repenting our sins –
In the Pass of Dafydd's sons,
And on up the wooded combe,
To glimpse her fine hair, I climb.
I muddle on in mist, grope
The fork of Gyfylfaen gap;
Where the valley opens fair,
I seek my girl, garbed in fur,
Elusive as a mirage.
Her stealth withholds her image
Though in my zeal I seek her
At Pant Cwcwll in summer.
At Castell Gwgawn I claw
Like a gosling searching straw
For grain. At Heilin's household,
I pant like a husky hound.

Below Ifor's court I crept
Like a monk who haunts a crypt,
Vainly seeking meetings with
Shy, coy, vanishing Morfudd .
Either side of Nant-y-Glo
There is no hill nor hollow,
No twist, no wind, no portion
That has not known my passion:
A second Ovid: I bawl

At Gwern-y-Talwrn (my call
She answered here once: a glimpse
She gave me – I got a glance
Beneath her gown). Here, I know,
There's a place where grass won't grow:
Here, like Adam, once I made
Our leafy bed in the glade.

Woe-betide the soul that walks
Chained to the body, and works
Without wages: poor the pay
When the body leads the way.

**Notes:** The poem makes reference to a number of places – some of which can still be found today – in the triangle of country between Aberystwyth, Tal-y-bont and Ponterwyd. Dafydd (and presumably his beloved Morfudd) spent his early days at Brogynin, and the modern village of Elerch is a little over a mile away. Cellïau'r Meirch was probably a homestead. Oral history evidence suggests that the current River Stewy was known as the Saleg in the early nineteenth century, and a record from 1937 attests that Bwlch Meibion Dafydd was a track leading from Brogynin to Elerch. Bwlch y Maen is a convergence of a number of paths two miles east of Elerch, changed to Gafaelfwlch y Gyfylfaen by Dafydd because of its consonance. The whereabouts of Pant Cwcwll is unknown, but Tal Pont Cuculh was given to the monastery of Strata Florida (Ystrad Fflur, Dafydd's most likely place of burial) in 1336. Castell Gwgawn was also given to the monastery, and has since vanished, at least by name. Nant-y-Glo is the name of a small farmstead half a mile from Brogynin. Ifor is a common mediaeval Welsh name, and the one mentioned here is not Dafydd's later patron, Ifor ap Llywelyn of Morgannwg – nor is the stream Bysaleg to be confused with Basaleg, the latter's home. The last four lines are an ironic reference to a mediaeval Welsh poetic tradition: the didactic dialogue between the body and the soul. Interestingly, Iolo Goch also parodied this tradition in a poem which took his reader on an imagined tour of the lands he travelled as a court bard.

## *The Funeral of the Poet, Killed Outright by Love*
Angladd y Bardd

Lily's pallor on your face,
Chaste as ice, you wear a lace
Of spiderweb to keep you chaste.
Mair! I'm doomed, and it's a waste!
Your family has sown fear
Within you, and I can't fare
Well. "Farewell" fits like a glove:
*(Gasp of unrequited love.)*

Fine, fickle girl, if you kill
One who calls you "perfect jewel",
Guilt shall be your sad token
When I lie dead and broken.
Leaves shall be my humble grave
In the lowly birchwood grove;
Ash-tips and birch-tops will read
A wind-voiced rite, and the Rood,
A crossed twig, will bless my shroud
Of clover, my pall a cloud
Of living leaves. The wild place
Will sing plaintive psalms of grace,
My bier: eight branches entwined
With flowers of lime and woodbine.

Seagulls from the ocean swell
Fly in thousands, bearing well
My bier, and a lilting breeze
Wafts me down a nave of trees.
Maiden-tresses of the birch
Are the windows of the church.
Like two icons framed with leaves,
Two nightingales sing of loves
Perished. Wreaths of wheat, stacks
Of wood, an altar of sticks,
Choirstalls of logs. Elm-seed jewels
Stud the floor, though the Jealous
One denies me. Birds are friars
Singing plainchant, and each phrase
Is perfect Latin, the leaves
Of their breviaries alive
With greenness. The organ plays:
A fresh wind amid the hay.

There in Gwynedd's birchwood glade
Lies my grave, all spilt with gold
Of sunlight. The nightingale's
Parish mourns. Muse of the groves,
The chantry cuckoo sings my soul
To sleep. Trees, flowers, soil
Offer orisons and psalms.
Roots are everlasting arms.

My Mass shall fill summer's months,
My soul aflight like white moths.
By God's grace the poet flies,
Spiralling to Paradise.

**Notes:** When Thomas Parry published his edition of the works of Dafydd ap Gwilym in 1956, he excluded this delightful poem from the canon on the grounds that the *cynghanedd* is imperfect in several of the lines (in other words, the consonantal repetitions do not follow the strict rules observed by many of the poems whose attribution to Dafydd is secure). However, there are some compelling reasons for questioning Parry's judgement. All of the eleven manuscripts attribute the poem to Dafydd. The poem shares the theme of the creatures of the woodland offering religious devotion with another of Dafydd's poems ('The Woodland Mass'), and like it, the poem teeters deliciously on the brink of heresy with its depiction of woodland birds performing the sacraments. There is also the unmistakable suggestion of Dafydd's lightness of touch in the subtle transition between the self-mocking over-dramatisation of the opening of the poem, and the lyrical beauty of its climax – unmistakable enough to suggest that if this is not the work of Dafydd himself, it is that of a talented and likeminded disciple. In a marvellous essay on 'Tradition and Innovation in the Poetry of Dafydd ap Gwilym', Rachel Bromwich argues that this poem was influenced by French "bird-debate" poems, and by one in particular which insists, as the poet does here, that the birds sing in Latin (Rachel Bromwich, *Aspects of the Poetry of Dafydd ap Gwilym*, Cardiff, 1986, pp. 77-78). However, as with Dafydd's appropriation of that other great French tradition, the *fabliau*, there is in this poem a lightness of touch and a tone of gentle self-mockery which has much in common with a number of other works by Dafydd ap Gwilym.

## *Disputing with a Dominican*
Pregeth y Brawd Du

The friar preaches diatribes
On deadly sin: this I despise.
Nought but bread within his nook,
The breviary his only book,
Berry-bald, lives like a wretch
And subsists on seeds of vetch,
In mousy habit, dank, drear,
Forever bending Mair's ear,
Bold protector when he spies
Motes in other people's eyes.

The friar's sermon: "Lad, forswear
Your pert maid with pretty hair,
She for whom you lilt in verse,
For time will lapse, cast its curse
On woman's wiles. Spend your days
Penning odes in God's praise.
The Lord's Prayer in seven pleas,
The Paternoster – keep to these
By Mair and Peter. Forthwith
Renounce the clamour of *cywydd*!"

Churl in habit like a hive
Of angry bees that sting and strive
To prod your pique: Friar's curse
To bear the brunt of Iolo's verse
With face as blue as berries. Stick
To bothering Saint Dominic,
Bliss of paradise to know –
Fly there like a black-winged crow
And clap your beak, your cowl raise
To ring your hollow bell of praise,
Tolling "Jesus" like the knell
That summons piebald friars to hell.
Tonsured crow who hides his vice
And caws, and prates of paradise,

Pious prig, pursue your mission
Of prudery and prohibition;
Heaven wither your grim heart,
But leave me to my loving art!

**Notes:** One manuscript attributes this poem to Madog Benfras (fl. 1320-60), but the other manuscripts do not cite an author. Friars were unpopular in fourteenth century Wales, because their preaching zeal was not always combined with exemplary living, and another poem (*Gwae fi na wyr y forwyn*) which certainly was the work of Dafydd ap Gwilym, lampoons a grey friar or Franciscan. As mentioned here, Dafydd's younger contemporary, Iolo Goch, also wrote two fierce satires against this order, and it is clear that the bards, who had so fervently embraced the traditions of courtly love, had every reason to resist the moralizing teachings of the Friars. The present poem tackles a Dominican, a member of the Preaching Friars, an order whose mission was to combat heresy through preaching, and ultimately through the Inquisition. In Wales, the friars tended to base themselves in the Marches and the royal boroughs, and were thus perhaps seen as an English incursion on Welsh spirituality. By the fifteenth century, however, friars had a bad reputation in England as well: a fact attested by the appearance of carvings of preaching foxes in friars' habits in church wood-carvings. The friars were also resented by the secular clergy because of their open competition for preferment and for offerings, but here, as elsewhere, the charge is also one of hypocrisy and spiritual pride.

## *The Sigh*
Y Uchenaid

A rasping, stertorous sigh
Is splitting my tunic awry:
An exhalation, frigid
As frost, shall rend my rigid
Breast. The quaking, baleful strain
Shall split me with searing pain.
From my pregnant, brooding breast,
Like the sigh of brainsick beast,
Comes a queer, dissonant note,
Constriction at my throat,
Commotion of recollection,
Candle's callous extinction,
Cywydd's vortex, cruelly spinned,
Cold barrage of misty wind.

When I am vexed, all presume
I'm a piper, as the fume
Comes snorting from my hollows
Loud as a blacksmith's bellows.
A sigh like this will make fall
A stone from a sturdy wall.
A roar to shake a man's length:
A girl's anger quakes my strength.
A withered cheek, wind-squall wet
Marks my autumn of regret.
This wild anger at defeat
Would hull oats or winnow wheat.
A year's anguish in this sigh:
Give me Morfudd, or I die.

**Notes:** The mark of Dafydd's authorship can be seen in the self-mocking overstatements and the somewhat hyperbolic agricultural metaphors.

# *The Penis*
Y Gal

By Christ, penis! I must guard,
Hand and eye, against your goad,
More staunch than ever, upstart pole
One lawsuit beyond the pale!
Complaint has come, you cunt-quill:
I must bridle you, or quail
Beneath the law, lout! Monstrous
Snout! Despair of all minstrels!

Rank rolling-pin, rising up!
Scrotum-horn upraised to romp
Around Christendom! You grind,
A pestle, in dark engrained,
Dragpole to a lurking snare,
Feathered gander set to snore
Away winter! Neck that jerks
Wetly, and slimily jacks
Itself upward toward its goal:
Primes its shaft to split a girl!
Hole-headed eel, poised to rim,
Hazel-pole, battering ram,
Thigh-length chisel set to gouge
Out a hundred nights, and gorge
Itself on flesh! Screw-threaded
Auger with a leather head!
Lustful crowbar, bent to burst
The lid-bolt of a girl's bare arse!
Tube-head whistle full of funk,
Set for blowing, steeled to fuck.
There's an eyehole in your pate
Deigns not to discriminate:
Finds all women fair, or cute:
Red-hot poker for a cunt.
Thatching-stick for a girl's groin,
Bell-clapper, gross, overgrown,
Grim whelp-maker, cause of kids,
Nostril with a crop of cods,
Trouserful of lewd thought
Wiry as a goose's throat,
Wanton pod, nail of hate,
White seed set to germinate.

Consider this, and hang your head,
Child-planter: you're out of hand,

Now I'm brought before the law.
Woe betide, and cower low!
I'm the master, prickface stinking!
Let the big head do the thinking!

**Notes:**. This is Dafydd's most explicit poem by far, and one which requires very little explanation. Despite the somewhat unusual subject, the poem does follow a number of established conventions observable in Dafydd's other work: the self-ironic tone, the string of increasingly adventurous metaphors, and the winding-up of a curse that comes perilously close to an invocation. The profanities are all Dafydd's own, but it should be noted that the word "cunt" ("cont" or "gont" in Welsh) was by no means as shocking then as it is to many people today. Like "arse", the word is used in a purely functional sense in Middle English texts, and even Hamlet makes puns on the word in the royal court of Denmark, admittedly whilst he is subject to a feigned madness. So pious a poet as Andrew Marvell still felt able to play on the word in 'To His Coy Mistress' without fearing any charge of crudity: he warns his intended that if she is not prepared to sleep with him, her virginity will eventually be taken away by worms, and "thy *quaint* honour turn to dust". A dragpole snare is a looped wire attached to a long heavy pole, or the trunk of a tree. Although it is still employed illegally by nefarious English gamekeepers, it is a particularly inhumane form of animal trap, and badgers regularly disembowel themselves endeavouring to escape. It is not known whether Dafydd really was subjected to lawsuits as a result of his amorous behaviour, or whether this poem was merely intended to entertain the more tavern-orientated portion of his clientele. In any case, the bawdy tradition has continued in Welsh verse to the modern day, and echoes of Dafydd's poem can perhaps be heard in Dylan Thomas's references to "the old ram rod" in his 'Lament' (1947).

# Satires

## Satire on Rhys Meigen
Dychan i Rys Meigan

Cretinous bungler, ass-bray – gormless clod,
Coy bum-sniffer of Gwalchmai,
Curs howl when he comes their way,
Curses dog him every day.

Consider Rhys Meigen: grim display – turd
Causing nausea. May he stray
Far, wayward dog, and stay
Away, cloying milksop of May.

Uncouth, deceptive, beast-grey – boaster
From Dyfi to Menai,
Chuntering, half-sized, splay-
Legged fake-in-the-making,

Coward who could never gain a lord's love,
Completely useless, it's plain,
He croons a vile wormwood strain,
Knavish ape, mouth like a drain,

Crude of tongue, corpse-cold brain – you blab
Flattery, and declaim,
Blatantly inviting blame,
Crappy beggar, spreading stain

Of crassness, crafty, pale, nasty bastard,
Boor on a course to fail,
Brazen braggart with baleful
Eyes. Mood: abrasive. Breath: stale.

Randy, crapulous *llatai* – getter of
Leprous ladies, craven pain
In the backside, shit-ingrained
Dog, paddle away, I pray.

His pantaloons look gay – coracle hides
Patched in motley. Its a strain
Getting him to write in plain
Welsh. Pen? Sword? He runs away.

Corpse-hackney, rotten hack-writer – filthy
Bard with lips that writhe
Like slugs. Men! Hide your wives!
His scuttling bugs will blight your lives.

From curdy mouth to clasping arse – his jaws
A clench of quarrels, fat farce,
His troughlike gullet set to fart
Verses, tettered travesty of art,

Nasty, blotch-legged, uncouth – with bulges
In his britches. Blessed, forsooth,
He who hangs the soup-wet youth,
Tomcat-stealthy, snide, uncouth,

Beer-drunken, slick of lip – squealing piglet –
He vomits, and lets it drip
On his fusty clothes. This
Codpiece of his, stained with piss,

Shows him up: a vagabond – and lice
Bite him on his shitten hand,
His hair: imp-trimmed. Taste: bland.
Lo! He comes, and blights the land.

Beam-legged, spindleshanked – no Cai Hir –
Battle-shy flatterer,
Sucker of rancid fat,
Neck like rawhide, face: flat

And leathery, like a worm – yeast-drinker –
Legs feeble as a lamb's,
Gut like butter badly churned,
Wire-haired, hankering for the womb.

He sang, feeble as a mouse – mischievous music
Rhyming rodent of the shithouse,
A composition any louse
Would blush to hear, the soused,

Pock-marked Rhys Meigen, courter of gallows.
Choose rope or banishment, or else you'll burn,
Maggot-footed, fat-basted travesty,
You gnash your green teeth, you rage, you gurn,
You cram your mouldy gob, you glutton,
Boar-gobbler, mutton-mouthed slurper, you turn
My stomach! Marrow-licker, slick drinker
Of rancid fat – I exorcise, by Cyndeyrn,
Your salmon-coloured, puckered lips, arse
Of greediness, engulfing all. I spurn
Your creamy-headed cock, coward-soldier
Standing at wonky attention. Dinbyrn
Scorns your lousy pelt, your vile, vulpine face,
Your complexion, fleshy and taciturn,

Your leech-like trousers, constipated flesh,
Your withered expression, your searching, stern
Lifeless eyes, your scurrilous snarl, scurrying,
Cat-clawed gait. Your meat-mashing mouth earns
No praise, drinker of dregs of sour cider
Made of crabs. Your fatuous, muck-fed face burns
Red as beetroot, as you bash out woeful
Awdls and englyns, glibly as you churn
Out crap into your britches. The tavern
Is emptied. You rave on, and never learn.

**Notes:** It is said that Dafydd composed this satire in response to an englyn written by Rhys Meigen, in which he claimed to have slept with Dafydd's mother. The tradition affirms that when Dafydd's satire was performed in front of him, Rhys dropped down dead. It is certainly true that many people believed that a well-penned satire could bring death on its victim, and the story is supported by a reference made by Dafydd in a debate with Gruffudd Gryg, in which he warns his rival: "be careful lest you end up twisted and dead, like Rhys, slain by poetry". However, it is more likely that this satire was really part of a comparatively normal ritual: the bardic debate, in which bards were expected to insult one-another inventively as a form of entertainment. Gwalchmai was a 12th Century court poet from Gwynedd, Cai Hir was King Arthur's prodigiously tall nephew, Cyndeyrn was a saint, and it is thought that Dinbyrn was a traditional Welsh hero.

# Poems of praise

## *Thanks for the Gloves*
Diolch am Fenig

Ifor's generous with gold:
There's no hand he does not gild
Ere it leaves his court. I dined
There yesterday, and was wined
Well enough to loose my tongue
In praise. Night leaves a lorn twinge
Of longing, for no wedding
Could coax a bride more willing
Than I am, though I travel
Afar. Praise is kind travail.

I came from his court with gloves
Money-filled to the gussets.
Ifor, patron of poets,
Gives his good gloves like a priest
Signing blessings, thick and fine,
Stuffed with coins, colour of fawn.
Oh, that I had penned a poem
Each time gold has crossed his palm,
Or coined *cywyddau* whenever
My finger touched his silver!

Fine girls always want – on loan –
My gloves. I've rehearsed my line:
"No." I'm never letting go
Of Ifor's gift, though they blow
Their pink cheeks out in disgust:
I am his devoted guest.
No ram-skin mitten will scour
My finger and leave a scar:
I wear deer-skin on each hand
From a benefactor's herd:
Gentle leather. I'll not let
Any weather get them wet.

By Rheged, I'll give him praise:
Great Ifor, who dwarfs his peers.
A second Taliesin,
Dafydd hones his lord's blessing
Out of words. I wish him health
As I stand before his hearth -
A place where men are brave, and maids
Chaste, possessed of noble minds,
Where even lords bend to bless
A mere bard with fond largesse,

Where every babe is well-borne,
Where hawks, hounds and wine abound,
Where garments are all scarlet
And no good poem stays secret.

In the Wennallt, not one tree
Has a head that is not green
In the wind alive and waving
With its neighbours interwoven.
So, a joyful throng is knit
At Basaleg: bard and knight
Bound to their Duke together -
And I shall serve no other.

No gloves for a Saxon fool -
No mere English gloves of wool:
Gloves of Ifor, perfect gift!
They fit my hand like a graft
Ingrowing. I wave: "All hail!"
In salute of Ifor Hael.

**Notes:** Like all mediaeval bards, Dafydd was not above unleashing a gush of fawning praise on a promising patron, but in the case of Ifor ap Llywelyn, who lived at Gwernyclepa, near to the village of Basaleg, the affection seems to have been quite genuine. It was Dafydd himself who gave Ifor his nickname: "Hael" (the Generous), and the poet was equally generous, composing no less than six poems in his praise. This is, in fact, the earliest surviving poem of thanks in the *cywydd* metre, and it seems likely that Dafydd's slightly younger contemporary, Iolo Goch – a still more effusive flatterer – was influenced by it. The hall of Rheged was the place where the sixth century poet Taliesin – the archetypal bard – sang the praises of his master Urien, and Dafydd is, of course, being quite as flattering to himself as he is to his patron in making the comparison. Craig y Wennallt was a woodland three miles to the north-west of Ifor's court.

## *Basaleg*

Get going, my lad, clad in green:
Through the birch wood be gone.
Go through Morgannwg. Know my mind:
Get to Gwynedd and drink mead.
Let this word be heard by men:
Splash it about the land of Môn.

Say this: I have been detained
Longer than I hoped or dreamed,
Not far from Cardiff, courting
A creature worth the catching.
By Solomon's song! No sleek,
Slender, soft-lipped girl in silk
Distracts me. Ifor's my goal:
More glamorous than any girl.
I rate him higher than sex, and
The love of stupid Saxons;
I won't wander, seek lovers,
But abide close to Ifor.
I won't stray; I'll never leave
Morgannwg while I'm alive.

Spawn of heroes, helmed with gold,
Noble, generous and good,
Hawk among a manly host,
Snugly seated on his horse,
First to victory in arms,
Falcon-wise in flights and charms,
Deathless stag, scourge of Deirans,
All men will find him dauntless.
His words are the ones I trust;
Other men are chaff and dust.

He puts rawhide in my hands
To ride with his matchless hounds.
His chalice will clash with mine,
All a-slop with Ifor's wine.
His stags take flight; I let fly,
Cast his hawks to wind and sky
At Basaleg, court of the strong,
Every mouth alive with song.
Any poet would aim for this:
To shoot arrows, join the lists,
Play blackgammon eye to eye
With a lord, play chess, and try
To mate him! We make wagers,

And both of us are winners:
Ifor puts me first. My voice
Strains to pay him back in verse.

Matchless largesse in his halls,
No man's valour's quite like his:
Modest Ifor: at his side
A poet, aglow with pride.

**Notes:** This poem is dedicated to Dafydd's friend and patron, Ifor ap Llywelyn, who lived in Gwernyclepa, near to the village of Basaleg, between Cardiff and Newport. Dafydd wrote many praise poems dedicated to wealthy patrons, and this is one of the most accomplished. He begins his *cywydd* – a verse form traditionally reserved for love-poetry – by lampooning his own customary device of the *llatai*, or love-messenger: for once the messenger is sent out to tell the world why the poet is not interested in courting a girl. Ifor's praise is sung through a series of conventional motifs – the comparison of the hero with stags and falcons, and with the heroes of the Gododdin, who fought against the Deirans – but the poet cannot resist a cheeky aside on the thought of beating his master at chess. The ironic reference to the Song of Solomon is evidence that the text was not always read allegorically in the Middle Ages: it is clear that Dafydd recognises it as a love-poem, and not as a parable about Christ and the Church.

## *Cywydd for Ifor Hael*
Cywydd i Ifor Hael

Ifor, all the stark splendour
Of stewardship, the grandeur
Of office, is mine. Lord of worth:
How my voice shall praise your wealth!

Brave as bronze – my praise boundless –
Great man, good man, and bounteous
With gold. I gave you strong words;
You paid in dark bragget: swords
Have less lustre. Your rhymer
Declaims your bright name: Rhydderch!
An armed man immune to wounds,
Friend to those who work in words:
When poets play upon harps
You bend your noble head to hear.

Vaunted, brave and valiant,
Never far from the vanguard,
Of noble lineage, devout,
No master was more deferent
To his poet, wise and grave:
Lord and bard are hand-in-glove.

I broadcast your fame abroad,
And return to Ifor, Lord
Most worthy of well-wrought words:
Truthful praises. Lips of bards
Trip to pronounce them: eight score
Myriad words of applause.
As far as man may travel,
As far as sun unravels,
As far as wheat is winnowed
As far as dew fills hollows
As far as unclouded eye
Can see – and three times as high –
As far as Welsh comes from lips,
Far as buds break at the tips:
Splendid Ifor, eyes ablaze,
I whet your sword, sow your praise.

**Notes:** In his fervour, Dafydd pays Ifor the enormous compliment of comparing him with Rhydderch Hael, one of the 'Three Generous Men' of the Welsh Triads (see Rachel Bromwich, *Trioedd Ynys Prydein*, Cardiff, 2006, pp. 5-7; 493-495.) Bromwich points out that the word "hael" probably possessed a more precise meaning than the English "generous", and may have been used to designate "a precise and recognised social status". The original Rhydderch Hael was a ruler of the northern Britons in the sixth century. Whatever associations the word carried for Dafydd and his patron, the name stuck, and Ifor ap Llywelyn was later referred to as Ifor Hael by other poets. Praise poems were a dime-a-dozen in mediaeval Wales, but Dafydd's rings with sincerity, the more so because he portrays Ifor as "Caeth y glêr" ("subservient to poets") – presumably implying that Ifor is so appreciated because he has a genuine taste for Dafydd's works, and goes to pains to hear them performed.

# Elegies

# *Elegy for Madog Benfras*
Marwnad Madog Benfras

A broken sieve that spills grain:
Such is life, and when it's gone
There's only dearth. The young lad
Who tonight is hale and glad,
Who lives a dream after birth,
Goes tomorrow into earth.

Nimble muse, why inspire,
Lead me down your path of fire
For Madog Benfras? A bard
Unequalled: a rhymer bold
Of pen: metre's warrior,
Word-joiner, englyn-worker,
Skilful *cywydd*'s conqueror,
Scansion's cunning carpenter,
Word grafter, vowel-honer
Crafter of odes to honour:
Songs of sociability,
Solos of sagacity.

A grim year it was that stole
Madog. Grief left us torn, still,
Mourning our wily thatcher
Of words, our glib-tongued teacher,
Peacock in a bardic gown,
Strutting in his high renown,
Yet guileless, slow to anger,
Sound-smoother, truthful auger,
Myrddin's peer in crafty words,
With wine-deep eyes, winning ways,
Summer's bell in month of May,
Trumping-horn before the play,
Song-burnisher, revelry-
Maker, lovely rivalry
Of harmonies, church organ,
Fine tribal poet-chieftain!

A dismal land: cold breath
Of poets stifling *cywydd* –
Golden talents were his pay,
Paupers now, the leaves of May,
Muffled tears fill the vale,
Mourn the tongue-tied nightingale.
The wood of birch, the ash grove,
Are in sere, bereft of love.

Verse-chapel, strong support,
Copper coin for woman-sport:
Death has done his boorish worst
And left the tuneless land a waste.
Woe to bards! Commend to God
Madog with his voice of gold.

**Notes:** It is very probable that Madog Benfras was still alive when this poem was written, since it was common practice for poets to compliment each other by exchanging elegies. Dafydd employs three metaphors in his descriptions of Madog's skills as a poet: the craftsman (and more particularly, the carpenter), the wizard, and the songster. It is probable that Madog and Dafydd were both accomplished musicians. The opening six lines have a wonderful stylistic economy in the original, and would stand today as an epigrammatical poem in their own right.

## *Elegy for Gruffudd ab Adda*
Marwnad Gruffudd ab Adda

When, by the lime-white wall,
Where apple trees grow well,
A nightingale by sun and star
Has sung, setting leaves astir,
With sweet, sustained song
And from her nest has slung
A gilded string of psalmody,
A gift of gleaming melody –
What dolour, what dismay
Should an archer wend his way
Within the whitewashed wall
And string his birch-bow well
And shoot, with wild abandon!
For though the apples burgeon
On each bough, no bard
Shall sing, but grieve the bird.

Powys, flowering land,
Where wine and music blend,
Was the orchard in the wall:
Now all good men bewail
Our nightingale of song.
A blue sword-blade swung,
Our gifted lad was killed,
Our cantref torn and cursed.
Three months, with no relief
Our unchallenged grief
Has vied with manly hate
For the sharp sword of fate.

Gruffudd, Addaf's son,
Sweetest bird of song,
As all good courtiers say,
The prince of budding May,
An organ, piping merry,
A songbird with a berry,
A bee upon a flower
Beneath Gwenwynwyn's tower.

What villainy, that a friend
In anger, sword in hand,
Should swing it in the wind
And give him his death wound!
Through the hair and skull

The weapon went, to spill
The brain that conjured words.
The blood gushed from the wound
That cleaved his yellow pate
And split his head apart:
The type of blow, I guess
You'd use to kill a goose.

His cheeks were gold and hale –
Our butchered nightingale.

**Notes:** Little is known of Gruffudd beyond the details set out in the poem, which many critics have regarded as a "fictitious elegy" in any case. They argue that the comparison of Gruffudd's killing with that of a goose smacks of "burlesque", but it seems to me that it hides a bitter anger: Dafydd is enraged that a great poet has been despatched perfunctorily, as a bird might be killed for the table. Three poems in Gruffudd's name have survived, and Rachel Bromwich maintains that his "superb cywydd to the uprooted birch-tree at Llandidloes... rivals the best of Dafydd's verse in its sensitive evocation of the personified tree's ability to feel and to suffer". If Dafydd knew the poet's work, it is difficult to see why he should choose to write a "fictitious elegy".

## *Rhydderch's Elegy*
### (on behalf of Llywelyn Fychan of Glyn Aeron)
Marwnad Rhydderch
(dros Llywelyn Fychan o Lyn Aeron)

Where slope of shale meets the skies
Yesterday I heard three cries
And cowered. I have known groans
Enough, but quaked to hear moans
Of mortal men, that rent the ground
In twain: pained, baleful sound
Like hunter's horn, vale to cloud.
No doom-bell ever clanged so loud.

What tone sings such doleful woe?
What pang of pain decrees it so?
Llywelyn Fychan lent his breath
To break word of Rhydderch's death,
His brother sworn. He lies in state
Within the court. Too fickle, fate!
As Amis grieved for Amiloun,
As torn mothers weep and swoon,
So, a man who loved his friend
Goes to ground and grieves his end:
Llywelyn's cry, a tolling knell,
A speechless word of what befell.

Rhydderch's lips, which kept their word
When giving wine – now interred –
Lie parted, dry, soon to perish.
Brought to dust, all I cherish:
Valour vanquished – shrivelled seed –
And rancid all of Rhydderch's mead
Slickly running down the drain.
Like a swan upon a chain!
So little stone it takes, to pave
The seven feet that make his grave.

Doleful sermon: that his worth
Lies subdued by dumb, thick earth.
All wealth of love, warmth of wit
Are gifts embraced by the pit:
Unstinting wisdom, worth and right,
Mirth and breath, and body white,
Values, virtues, nature's gift,
Learning, yearnings, largesse, thrift,
Charm and fame, and talk and song.

All have been, and all are gone.

What a tumult in the soil
When knight succumbs to sexton's toil.
Rest to Rhydderch! Spade the clod
With love and sweat. Trust to God.

**Notes:** This elegy was written for Rhydderch ab Ieuan Llwyd of Glyn Aeron in Ceredigion, a lawyer, administrator, patron of poets, and perhaps most importantly of all, the owner of the White Book of Rhydderch: surely one of the most important manuscripts in literary history, given that it is one of the two volumes which contain the original tales from the *Mabinogion*. Ironically, this extraordinary expression of grief for the passing of a knight and patron (written two centuries before the gravemaker scene in *Hamlet*) was almost certainly a *marwnad ffug* – an elegy written long before the death of the subject – since Rhydderch was still alive in 1391, more than ten years after the last poems written by Dafydd ap Gwilym. Surprising as it may seem today, such a practice was not uncommon in the century of the Black Death, when elegies for the great (like modern obituaries) were often required at a moment's notice. Dafydd's authorship is undisputed, and his hand can certainly be seen in the dark humour of the fourth-last line. Amis and Amiloun (Amlyn am Emig) were heroes of a Middle English romance, which is known to have been translated into Welsh in the fifteenth century, but Dafydd uses Welsh forms of their names, which suggests that he must have read an earlier translation, now lost. Iolo Goch appears to have had access to the same text, since he also uses the Welsh versions of their names. For an affordable version of the romance of Amis and Amiloun in Middle English, see Jennifer Fellows (Ed.), *Of Love and Chivalry: An Anthology of Middle English Romance*, London, 1993, pp. 73-145.

## *Elegy for Dafydd ap Gwilym*
by Iolo Goch

Yesternight when Dafydd died
A yawning morn of dolour dawned;
A knot of minstrelsy untwined,
In waking Wales a gaping wound.
Praise-shaper, bard of wonder,
Girl-blesser, abbess-wooer,
Craftsman of the silken word,
Cuckold-maker of his weird,
Hawk of girls, baiting lasses:
Constricting codes, taut jesses,
Cannot constrain tiercel-flight
Gyring, stooping, swooping light,
And crooked-clawed for catching love:
Words to take the prey alive
And turn her, at a soaring height,
Into the falcon of his heart.

I am a dog! Poet damned!
A world bereft of him is doomed
To live at a slower rate:
Dafydd sang; I merely prate,
Respectable and refined.
He the core, I the rind,
He the seedling, I the husk,
He the dawning, I the dusk,
I the pilferer of praise,
He the thrush who with no pause
Pours out songs into the wind:
His pinions hope, bill a wand
Of changing, making girls gold,
Raising bowers out of mould.
Roebuck's antler, sharp of tine,
Salmon-scale, borne of brine,
Jackdaw-jester, raven's craw,
Fiend of love, delight of war –
A path of thorns lies ahead
Now that vision's voice is dead.
Pale Morfudd of mourning brow
Only Mair can claim him now.

**Notes:** I began by paraphrasing Iolo Goch's elegy for the great bard, but could not penetrate the rather formal style of the surviving poet, who was about ten years younger than Dafydd. The thirteenth line of Iolo's elegy invokes the image of the "hawk of girls", but instantly drops it again; I have chosen to sustain it for the rest of the first verse paragraph. Iolo praises Dafydd's learning, but accuses him of "presumption" at one point. It is clear that Iolo did not know Dafydd at all well on a personal level, even though the former was the inheritor of the cywydd verse form which Dafydd pioneered. I have replaced most of Iolo's stately praises in the second verse paragraph with images of Dafydd's own, and in view of my own exceedingly minor status as a poet, have, I hope, lent the poem a humility which the original seems to lack. This is not to suggest that Iolo was not a supreme wordsmith. His own 'Description of a Girl' must surely have brought a smile to Dafydd's face, assuming that he lived to read it.

210

# Epilogue

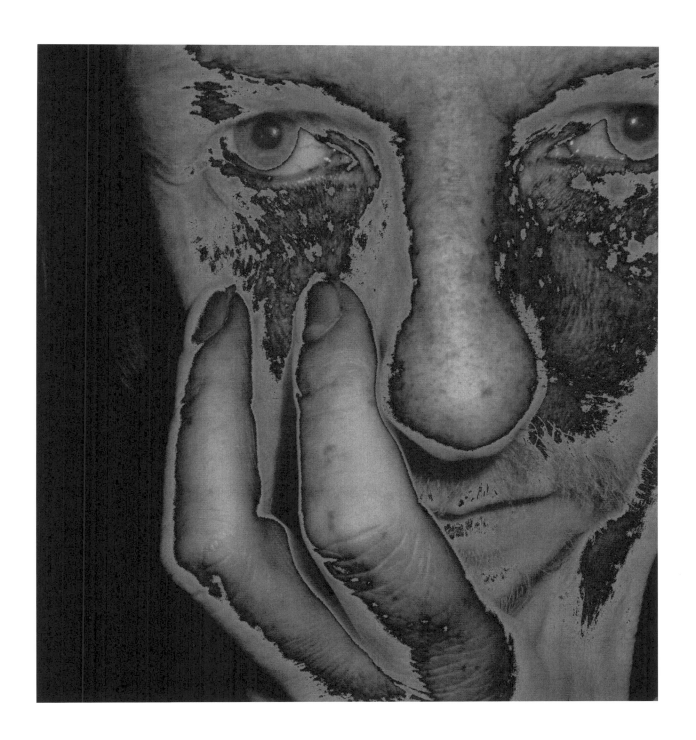

## *Recanting*
Edifeirwch

I gave my love, life and voice
To Morfudd, costly as verse
Wrung out like migraines – bounty
Of pain, born of cruel beauty,
My brow all ridge and furrow,
Her hair my noose of sorrow.
When death, with its blunt arrows
Parts my bones, threshes, harrows
Me in, then my stupendous
Ending will leave men speechless.

Lest pained lamentations rend
The air: Mair, and God, and Rood,
Forgive my loving – and sin.
Amen. I'll stop, and not sing.

**Notes:** Rachel Bromwich tellingly describes this poem as "semi-penitential". It echoes the tone of deathbed poems by earlier authors, but it is difficult to avoid the impression of a bitterness which works in opposition to the apparent purpose of the poem. It is widely believed that Dafydd ap Gwilym died of bubonic plague.

## *Acknowledgements:*

I am deeply grateful to Jeannie Howard, who offered me endless support in my pursuit of this project, and to Huw Davies and Dennis Roth, whose comments on my work in progress were invaluable. My professional colleagues and friends – especially Linda Sutton, Sarah House, Charlotte Kitching, Henry Bew, Sarah Beadle, Holly Leach and Claire Stark – have also been a source of encouragement and inspiration. At the outset, I might never have begun the paraphrasing project without the influence of Kathryn Wheeler, whose passion for music equals mine for poetry. Recordings of the works of singer and songwriter Robin Williamson have constantly been in my CD player in the course of the ten years I have spent on these paraphrases, and no one has done more to attune my ear to Celtic cadences. Finally, I am indebted to the Master Poet himself, for being as alive as ever in the twenty-first century.

All translations and pictures © Giles Watson, 2012.

Printed in Great Britain
by Amazon.co.uk, Ltd.,
Marston Gate.